30 Years of Grimsby Writers

30 Years of Grimsby Writers

Short Stories and Poems

Compiled by Jackie Collins

Contents

PROLOGUE

Thirty Years of Grimsby Writers

Pauline Murdoch

(Pauline is our longest-serving member)

I first attended Grimsby Writers in the 1990s. The meetings were held upstairs in Grimsby Central Library on a Monday evening. The leader at the time was a young man called Michael Bates. Maria Garner was the next leader. We were a lively group of about twenty or so. Some of us wrote prose and some wrote poetry.

Amyon was a member who contributed lots of poetry. The poets in the group started up a separate club called Driftnet Poets which ran for many years and was very successful.

June Baxendale, from her wheelchair, took over the writers' leadership, even having social events in her first-floor flat.

After June came Ron Geddes. Ron was Australian. He put a lot of emphasis on grammar.

We moved around a bit. We met at St Hugh's Church Hall, Grimsby Minister, Scartho Community Centre and latterly the Community Hub/Library in Scartho.

Our present leader is Jackie Collins. We have a wide variety of interesting sessions including guest speakers. We try our hand at short stories, poetry, including Haiku and, amongst other things, autobiography.

Many people have attended Grimsby Writers over the years. We have always been a happy group, sharing our work and also partaking in social events, meals out, competitions, writing courses, etc.

Some of us have had books published, plays performed and won prizes. At Queen Street Resource Centre, a group called 'Voices Talk, Hands Write' was led by Grimsby Writers and Driftnet Poets (including Maggie and June). It encouraged young people with intellectual disabilities to put their thoughts on paper. Talents were uncovered.

After 30 years of writing (for some of us) we present to you a little book of some of our stories and we hope you will enjoy reading it.

To Anyone Who Has an Itch

Ian Walker

(Ian is the newest member of Grimsby Writers as of Jan 2025)

I attended my first Grimsby Writers meeting in September 2024. I was retired and now had time to spend on activities that interested me. Although I wasn't a writer, I had enjoyed writing a few poems in my fifties, and thought that there was the potential that I'd enjoy the creative process of writing.

I was warmly welcomed into the group which consists of 15 or so like-minded people who like to write. During our fortnightly meetings, we get to write and share within the group short pieces of prose or poetry based on a specific theme. This is both challenging and entertaining. It is interesting to hear the variety of writing that can be elicited from a single simple theme. We also have guest speakers who discuss specific aspects of writing, which is very informative and useful to someone who does not have a writing background.

When I attended that first meeting, I was surprised to discover that we were being asked to provide short stories or poems to be included in an anthology celebrating 30 years of Grimsby Writers. I had not written fictional prose since my schooldays in the 1970s. Although this was a challenge for me, it was an enjoyable one. I found myself using parts of my brain that had been dormant for many years.

I hope that you enjoy the writings that I and other members of Grimsby Writers have produced within this anthology. I can thoroughly recommend the group *to anyone who has an itch* to write. You will be made very welcome and, who knows, maybe you're a successful author just waiting to be found!

30 Facts to Commemorate 30 Years of Grimsby Writers

Diane Hersey

In 2024 Grimsby Writers will celebrate 30 years of creativity, originality and imagination, as current members continue to share their passion for the written word. Therefore, exploring other great achievements that celebrate 30 years of longevity seems only fitting. To commemorate such milestones not only for Grimsby Writers but for the entertainment industries of music, motion picture and television. Politically and culturally, 1994 was a particularly eventful year with so many stand-out events taking the world by storm. Along with numerous trivialities which are stored in the archive of time.

At the top of each story in this book, you will find an actuality (fact) about 1994. The year the group started.

Diane, who contributed this section to the book found 30 facts for 30 years. Those that have not been fitted in above the stories are listed below. Thank you, Di, and thank you for your contribution to organising social events and baking cakes for us.

Tony Blair won the Labour Party leadership election in 1994, paving his way to becoming prime minister in 1997.

Woodstock '94, New York. An estimated 350,000 people attended.

The Lion King hit cinema screens. (Hakuna Matata.)

Schindler's List was released in the UK. A Spielberg film about how Oskar Schindler saved many Jewish refugees from the Holocaust.

The PlayStation was launched.

The Duchess of Kent became the first Royal in over 300 years to convert to Catholicism.

Harry Styles, British singer and actor was born.

Jackie Kennedy/Onassis died suddenly of cancer.

Ayrton Senna, Brazilian Formula One driver, died in a crash on the track in Italy.

Richard Nixon, former US President died.

The next four examples are a little different and celebrate the number 30

Bingo Calls:

Blind 30, Dirty Gertie, Burlington Bertie and Speed Limit.

And last of all, 30 years of marriage is recognised as the Pearl Anniversary.

STORIES & POEMS

1994 - The National Lottery made its first draw live on BBC 1.

Robot Type 30

Dave Bromley

Almar Luckheart considered himself lucky to have been born in the 2020s, a member of Generation W. He could not imagine what it had been like for his forbears, who must have had a wretched life. He had seen an auto film of people having to go outside to work, shop or for education. Those were the dark days twenty years ago before The Great Overseer and the Advance Party overthrew democracy and assumed power, heralding a new world where every man or woman was the master of technology, not the servant.

Like most of his generation, Almar worked a three-day week from home. His home was a government-supplied, standard-equipped, solo person living pod with one main room, a sleeping area, and a small shower and toilet room. Almar's link with the outside world was through his master computer, which he used for his work, shopping and socialising with his online colleagues. Only last week, he and three others had a four-way online video camera chat for twenty minutes. He rarely left the pod because he believed the outside world was a dangerous and frightening place,

One of the first changes the Advance Party made was to abolish income tax, which proved a popular move, and it was replaced with a compulsory State Lottery. Each adult member of society had to purchase a certain number of tickets each week, dependent upon their income. The majority considered the lottery a good idea though they paid more for tickets than before as income tax. The Advance Party frowned upon cash prizes; instead, the prizes were composed of technical items such as computers and robots.

For fifteen years, since his eighteenth birthday, Almar had bought his tickets, but the only prize he had ever won was five free tickets in the next weekly draw. Today, he discovered, by auto message, that he had won this week's star prize. The message did not tell

1

him the prize he had won but informed him the lottery organisers would advise him later.

Almar could not concentrate on anything after he had received the message, and every few minutes would go to the screen to see if another message had arrived. He tried to remember what the top prizes had been. One week, it had been the latest Musk Super Comm 3D reality transposer, which sounded fantastic, although he had yet to discover what a transponder did. Another week, the prize was a Holo Player, which would play any song you wanted and generate a hologram of the artist performing in your pod. Almar quite liked the idea of that prize. Although, to be honest, Almar was not worried about what the prize would be, as the Great Overseer had said in one of his speeches, 'It is not the taking part, but the winning that is important.'

Three hours later, Almar's computer screen lit up, and a message scrolled across the screen.

'This week's Star Prize is a Robot Type 30.'

When he read the message, Almar had to sit down; he thought this was unbelievable. The Type 30 was the latest, most advanced robot on the market. He had heard about it on the 'What's New' podcast. A few minutes later, another message appeared on the screen.

'A drone will deliver your prize tomorrow morning.'

Almar usually had no trouble sleeping; the soft, hypnotic music and calming aroma of spring flowers from an electric blower wafting over his bed would have him asleep in minutes, but tonight, he lay, eyes wide open. The excitement was almost too much to bear, despite never thinking about getting or ever wanting a robot before. As Almar lay thinking, he had to admit for the first time that he occasionally felt isolated, and the robot could provide a kind of companionship. He knew such a thought was mistaken and he could never admit it out loud. It would mean serious trouble for him if the Great Overseer heard him say such blasphemy. After his sleepless night, the first thing Almar did once the automatic lights came on to herald the start of the day was to go to the computer screen. A message awaited him.

'Your drone delivery is due at 10.33 hours.'

Almar looked at his Ever-So-Smart Watch; another two hours and eight minutes to wait. Drones were always on time. While having breakfast, an A2 energy drink, he began to have doubts. Was this some big wind-up, perhaps one of his online colleagues laughing at his expense? He kept looking at his watch, and as it got nearer the appointed time he had persuaded himself it had been a joke of some kind and not a hilarious one at that. Despite his growing doubts, he could not help but keep looking at his Ever-So-Smart watch every few minutes. Time seemed to move slowly, much slower than ever before. But, as the digital watch flicked from thirty-two to thirty-three minutes past the hour, a message appeared on his screen.

'Your package has been delivered.'

Perhaps it had not been a hoax, and he had won the prize. Almar made his way to the pod's front access panel and, looking at the image from the external security camera, saw his Robot Type 30 for the first time. It was human shape, only four feet tall, with two arms, two legs, a rotund body, and a featureless globe head covered in white plastic. When Almar pressed the release button, and the front access panel opened, the robot moved forward and entered the pod. Once inside, it did a slow 360-degree turn as if inspecting the space before stopping in front of his new master.

"It is tiny, is it not?" said the Robot

"I beg your pardon."

"Your pod. Should I have said small? I expected something much larger and grander. I hardly consider this a suitable establishment for a robot of my specifications and power."

"I'm very sorry about that. I didn't need a robot, but I have won you, so we had better both make the best of it. What should I call you?"

"I am Robot Type 30."

"That is too much of a mouthful," said Almar. "I shall simply call you Thirty."

"As you wish and I shall call you Master. That is the name installed in my control system."

That seemed to end that conversation, and Almar was at a loss to know what to do or say next. After a long pause, Thirty said. "What do you wish me to do first, Master?"

"I don't know. There is not much to do. Oh, I know, you could make my bed."

"Make your bed, that I will do," said Thirty and moved across to the sleeping area.

Arriving at the bed, the robot extended his arms, lifted the bed in the air, and began pulling it apart.

"What are you doing?" Almar shouted.

"What you asked me to do, Master. Making you a bed, but first I must pull this one apart to make space for the one I make," said Thirty.

"When I said make the bed, I didn't mean build me a new one."

"I have done wrong, Master?"

"You most definitely have," said Almar.

It had not been a good start. Almar and Thirty took over an hour to get the bed back close to its original state. After this, they ignored one another for the rest of the day. Thirty stood sulking in the pod's corner, and Almar tried to get on with some work and catch up with what he should have done yesterday. Only when it got close to the hour that the Great Overseer had designated as the time to retire for the night that Thirty spoke again.

"Is there no task you wish me to perform, Master?"

"No, just stay where you are while I go to what remains of my bed and try to get some sleep."

"Excellent, Master."

Surprisingly, Almar slept well, but had a nightmare of his pod being invaded by an army of Robot Type 30s. The following morning, when Almar came out of the sleeping area, he found Thirty standing by the front panel.

"What are you doing, Thirty?"

"I have been guarding during the night. Protecting you against intruders," said Thirty.

"That is very good of you, but I have never had an intruder."

"There is always a first time, and it is one of my tasks to guard you."

"Fine, if you want to, but I am now going to...," Almar paused and stopped himself saying, "take a shower," remembering the bed incident, and continued, "have a shower."

"Excellent, Master," said Thirty.

The shower in Almar's pod was very effective. A powerful jet with water at the temperature he liked descending upon him. He was pouring shampoo on his hair when the shower door crashed open and Thirty came in. A naked man can feel very vulnerable in front of a robot, even one that is only four feet tall.

"Get out!" screamed Almar.

"I thought you would like your back scrubbed."

"I do not. Now, get out"

"Shall I get your breakfast ready?"

"Yes, do that, but get out."

When Almar came out of the shower room he was still shaking, whether out of fear or anger, he was unsure.

"Breakfast is served," said Thirty

Almar could see a bowl of cereal on the table and smelt sausages and bacon frying.

"What is this? I only have a glass of A2 for breakfast," said Almar.

"That is not enough to start a day. It would help if you had a balance of protein, carbohydrates, and fats," said Thirty.

Later, Almar realised this was the turning point. He should have stood his ground, but the smell of food cooking was irresistible, and he gave in to Thirty. The cooked breakfast, the first he had eaten since childhood, he had to admit, had been delicious.

Thirty took more control over Almar's life and habits as the weeks passed. On the plus side, they would spend pleasant evenings together watching old films and TV shows on the video screen. Thirty was very keen to watch a series from the last century called Doctor Who. Almar also found the program entertaining but wished that after it finished, Thirty would not move around the room, shouting, "Exterminate, exterminate!"

It didn't take long to realise that having Thirty was a mixed blessing. One task Almar hated was placing the online order for the supermarket. There was always an online queue, which meant waiting, and almost inevitably the person in front would have hundreds of special offer coupons that needed to be processed. The solution, he thought, was to give the job to Thirty. The next day, the order arrived, consisting of 50 bananas, 100 toilet rolls, and a carrot. Almar realised it had not been such a good idea. Another time, while waiting on the computer screen for instructions from Head Office, Almar said to Thirty, "I'm waiting for a message." And the next thing he knew was being face down on the keyboard with Thirty slapping his back. Thirty claimed he thought his master had said he wanted a massage.

Almar was also beginning to notice a change in the master-robot relationship. Thirty was becoming bossy, insisting Almar only ate certain foods and exercised. The robot also demanded they only watch shows Thirty liked on the video screen. And then the shower door, always having to be locked to prevent Thirty from bursting in, wanting to scrub his back. Almar was getting close to the age when he could cohabit, which the Great Overseer had decreed was thirty-five. Over recent years, he has become very fond of one of his social media colleagues, Virtue. She was a few years younger, but that was alright because females could cohabitate once they reached twenty-six. But how would she react to Thirty?

One evening, whilst watching the video screen, Almar told Thirty about his desire to cohabitate with Virtue. The robot agreed that was a good idea and offered to kidnap the girl and bring her to the pod. Almar quickly rejected the offer, and the conversation finished because an episode of 'Fools and Horses,' another of Thirty's favourites, was beginning. When you are used to living alone, having anyone else in your life, even a robot, can be disruptive. The final straw came when Almar was on a video call to Virtue. He told the girl how much he liked her and would like to cohabit with her when permitted.

"But I don't know you. What are you like?"

With this, to his horror, Almar saw a naked picture of himself in the shower. Until then, he hadn't realised that Thirty had filmed everything twenty-four hours a day and could recall and relay it to social media. Not only had the image gone viral, but had been shared with his other two hundred social media colleagues. Thirty's plea, that he thought he was helping Almar, did not save him. The robot would have to go. The only problem was how to get rid of him. A search on the celestial web had the answer.

"All robots have a small panel on their backs that gives access to the microcontroller box. It comes in two parts pushed together. Pull them apart, and it turns the robot off."

Almar went around the back of Thirty and opened the panel. Shouting the words, "Exterminate, exterminate!" he pulled the controller box apart. Thirty toppled and then, with a bang, fell to the floor.

***

Three weeks later, Thirty still lay on the floor where he had fallen. Almar had heard nothing from Virtue, and she had taken him off her colleagues list. Quite a few of his other colleagues who had received the image of him in the shower had also un-colleagued him. These were dark days for Almar as a blanket of depression fell over him.

A new message from the robot manufacturers appeared on his screen one morning.

"We have lost contact with your Robot Type 30. Please ensure that its communication unit has not been detached. We have discovered bugs in the software program, which may have caused

some robotic units to run erratically. We have a software Type 31 update we wish to download to resolve this issue."

Almar sat staring at the screen for some time. Then he turned and looked at Thirty, just an unmoving collection of sensors, actuators, and an electro-conductor. Had he been that bad and intrusive? Yes, he had, but was Almar missing his company? Yes, he was. He rose, walked across to the inert object on the floor, and, turning the robot over, opened its back panel.

"This is your last chance," said Almar, as he reconnected the microcontroller and closed Thirty's back panel. Then a whirring sound resonated around the pod, and the robot bounced upright.

"I am sorry, Master. I must have had a power loss, but I am fine now. Robot Type 31 ready for orders. What. Do you wish me to do now?"

"I have some work to do, and while I do that, I would like you to clean the pod thoroughly."

"And then, Master?"

"And then we will sit down and watch Dr Who."

"Very good, Master." And with that, Robot Type 30 deep-cleaned the pod until it was spotless. However, Almar would have preferred it if the robot had not gone around the pod, exclaiming, "Exterminate, exterminate!" all the time. To shut him up, Almar said, "What should I call you now, Thirty or Thirty-One?"

"I am Thirty and you are my friend, Almar," said the robot.

Friend. Almar had never had a friend before. Colleagues, yes, but never a friend. The Great Overseer did not approve of such relationships, he considered they reduced efficiency and everyone knew efficiency was the driving force of the state. Without obedience and efficiency, man and womankind would fall apart. But the idea of a friend appealed to him, someone to confide in and enjoy their company. Yes, he and Thirty would be friends.

Afterwards, when he settled down to watch Dr Who, Almar had to admit that the new Thirty was a real improvement with the bugs removed. Yes, it hadn't been a bad day, especially as Virtue had sent him a video message. While Thirty sat in front of the video screen, enthralled by Dr Who and the Daleks, Almar was deep in thought. If he and Virtue co-habited, he would have to apply for a multi-person pod big enough for three? And who knows, if Virtue cohabited, might it not become four or five in time?

"Thirty, what are you like at babysitting?" asked Almar when the program had finished.

"I don't know, Master. I have never sat on one, but I could try if you wish."

The answer shocked Almar, but then he heard a strange chortling noise he had not heard before. Looking across at Thirty, whose body was shaking, he realised the robot was laughing. The latest upgrade must have given the robot a sense of humour.

"You plonker, Thirty," said Almar and they both began laughing

Whether that was good or bad, only time would tell. But one thing was certain. Almar and Thirty were stuck with each other, like it or not. And all things considered, Almar certainly did like it. He liked it very much.

1994 - Wet, Wet, Wet's, Marti Pellow's "Love Is All Around" topped the UK single charts for 15 weeks.

Heaven-Sent Valentine

Janet Chamberlain

Hayley stared around the glittering ballroom. This was a mistake. A huge mistake. What had made her, a humble housekeeper, think she could blend into this world of rich, sophisticated people?

The idea had come to her on her thirtieth birthday, when she'd found a crumpled ticket to a *Grand Valentine's Ball* wedged behind her employer's bin. She'd smoothed it out, suddenly feeling ridiculously excited. She could do the right thing and toss it into the rubbish where it obviously belonged… or see it as a heaven-sent opportunity to bring some glitz and sparkle into her life, and show her friends and cheating ex-fiancé that she was doing brilliantly without him. Imagine their expressions, when they saw her pictures on social media!

And if her employer saw them too?

Chances were, she wouldn't care. Recently split from her live-in boyfriend, her employer had jetted off on an adventure holiday, leaving a team of decorators to transform her home, and Hayley on-call to give the place a thorough post-decorating clean.

Which was fine. Hayley was glad of the extra money, but her employer's spontaneity had made her see her own life for what it was — dull, predictable, and boring.

She heaved a weary sigh. Money had been tight since her ex had left, but with careful budgeting she'd been able to take over the flat they'd shared and pay all the bills. A huge weight off her mind, but it had meant no fun nights out for the foreseeable future. Not even on her birthday. So there she was at the milestone age of thirty, with nothing to celebrate or get excited about.

Even if she'd had enough money for a night out, her friends wouldn't have been game. All married with young families, they didn't have time for much more than a few hurried texts these days. Her ex, on the other hand, had married the woman he'd cheated with and the two of them were always off on some fun getaway, paid for by his new in-laws.

Not that she envied him. At least not the rich in-laws part. What little money she had, she'd earned, and wouldn't want things any other way. But sometimes she longed for the chance to do something fun and exciting.

She looked down at the crumpled ticket. She'd been doing the right thing for as far back as she could remember, and all it had got her was a cheating ex and a lonely existence. Maybe it was time to break the habit and take a few risks?

The next day she set to work making a dress for the ball – a deep red, elegant dress, inspired by a celebrity photo in one of her employer's magazines. It took a while, but once it was finished, she had to admit it was well worth the effort. As long as she kept her cool, no one would know she didn't belong.

She didn't feel very cool now, though. Everyone stood around in close-knit little groups and love-struck couples. Where were the lively singles, eager to make new friends? She gazed frantically around the room, looking for someone – anyone – who might be up for a chat.

Her gaze landed on the last two people in the world she wanted to see right now – her ex and his wife – heading her way at a very determined pace.

They paused in front of her.

'Hello,' she said, trying her best to sound nonchalant. 'Fancy seeing you here.'

Slowly, her ex looked her up and down. 'Just what I was thinking.' He smiled. 'Nice outfit, by the way.'

Her mouth went dry. Had he realised she'd made it from the bedroom curtains?

His barely contained laughter said that he had, and was about to share this observation in a voice no one could fail to hear. She had seconds to get away before she died of embarrassment. But how? She couldn't just run out the door. That would seem desperate and pathetic.

She glanced towards the bar. Maybe she could gatecrash one of the small groups there – if only to ask directions to the ladies.

It was then that she noticed the man sitting alone at the end of the counter. A gorgeous, dark-haired man, whose equally gorgeous wife or girlfriend would probably appear any minute. But right now, he was her only chance to escape humiliation.

She took a deep breath and looked her ex directly in the eye. 'Thank you – can't stop, I'm afraid. Boyfriend waiting at the bar.'

Then, without looking back, she ran across the floor, perched on the stool next to Mr Handsome Stranger, and touched him lightly on the arm. 'Please, please pretend you know me,' she whispered. 'Just for a couple of minutes.'

'Happy to oblige,' he whispered back. 'Take all the time you need.'

A sigh of relief whooshed past her lips. 'Thank you. My ex is behind me with his new wife.' Blind panic made her share more than she intended. 'And I really, really don't want them to know I'm here on my own.'

'No problem,' he answered, 'and if it's any consolation... I'm here on my own, too.'

Her heart leaped. 'You are?'

A pause, as if he were deciding how much he should tell her. He looked down into his glass. 'I lost my wife a couple of years ago and coped by taking on extra work. Coming here tonight was my friends' idea. They said I needed to get out of my rut.' He raised his gaze and smiled. 'Although looking round, I'm not sure it's my type of thing.'

'Me neither,' Hayley told him. 'I didn't realise everyone here would be part of a couple.'

He placed a hand on her arm. '*Almost* everyone. I'm Mark by the way. How would you feel about the two of us helping each other out and seeing this through together?'

Hayley stared into his deep brown eyes. 'I-I'd like that very much.'

As the night progressed and they danced and twirled under the glitter ball, Hayley had more fun than she'd ever imagined.

But after the final slow dance, a shadow crossed Mark's face. 'I like you, Hayley; more than I've liked any woman for a long while, but...' He paused as if he was struggling to find the right words. 'I'm afraid one of us... hasn't been completely honest.'

Her heart dropped down to her shoes. Had her ex waylaid him in the gents? Told him she didn't belong here and planted the idea she was out to snag a rich man? She swallowed hard, fighting back the tears. How could she make him understand she wasn't like that?

Truth was, she couldn't.

'The thing is,' he went on, avoiding her gaze. 'I'm... not the person you think I am.'

Wait – this was about *him?*

'What I said about losing my wife; all that was true, but I'm not well off, like you and all these people here. I work as a painter and decorator and would never normally come to an event like this.'

'So why...?'

'Because I found the ticket in a client's bin and let my workmates talk me into using it.' His face clouded. 'I don't belong here, Hayley – my dinner suit came from a charity shop, for heaven's sake – and when I look at you, all sparkling and beautiful in your expensive designer gown, I know we're too different to ever be together... however much I might want it.'

Wow. Just wow! Her first instincts had been right. That ticket was truly heaven-sent. She felt like singing and dancing all at once.

'This client...' she said, pretty sure she already knew the answer. 'Had she recently split with her boyfriend and gone off on some wild adventure holiday?'

A look of puzzlement crossed his face. 'Yes, I believe she had, but how –'

'Did I know?' She took his hand and clasped it tight. 'I like you too, Mark, I really do, and believe it or not, we have far more in common than you might think.'

She indicated the empty table next to them. 'Let's sit down, and I'll tell you all about it.'

1994 – Forrest Gump was released, with Tom Hanks and the saying, "Life is like a box of chocolates."

Super Gran

Jacqueline Collins

I studied Sid's photo on the mantelpiece beside his gold retirement clock. "I miss you, Sid," I said, "even more so during this Covid lockdown. It's so lonely and boring here in the retirement village. And because we're vulnerable we have to stay in." I couldn't help the sigh. "If I watch any more TV, I swear I'll get square eyes."

I could almost see Sid nodding in sympathy. "So I've come up with an idea," I rushed on. "It might sound silly, but I'm going to close my eyes, draw three quick circles in the air, and stab my index finger at that open page of the telephone directory on the table. I'll ring whatever number I point to and maybe find someone new to chat with. Here goes, no looking at the name, just close the book and dial the number 01739 303030"

As my quivering finger pressed the digits, I broke out in a cold sweat but forced myself to continue. I had to end the loneliness, and this phone call was my best chance. "0 7 7 3 9 3 0 3 0 3 0. There! All done."

An exasperated male voice answered, "About bloody time, Alfie, lad."

"It's not Alfie, I'm afraid."

"Bottled it again, has he? Frankly, Lady, I don't care who you are as long as you can drive. You've got the car, right?"

"I have a car."

"Lady, we've not got time. Listen, park as close as you can to the main entrance of the bank on Cotswold Street. At precisely 1 pm unlock the boot and doors - and start the engine. When three men are in, drive off. Remember to dump your phone."

The line went dead. I checked Sid's clock, 12.20 pm. I gave his photo the look, which meant I had a dilemma, and we needed to talk.

His voice came to me, *Gertie, old girl, it's an adventure. Don't overthink it.*

"Four in one car breaks the Covid rules, Sid."

You've had both your jabs, Gertie, old girl, go for it. The village won't have seen this much excitement in years!

"Shall I? The police wouldn't arrest a harmless little old lady. I'll explain, I got a request for a lift on my phone, it sounded urgent, so I responded. OK, Sid, I love you."

I love you too Gertie.

It's 12.25 pm. I need my warm coat, driving shoes, and driving glasses. Into a holdall, I throw a 24-hour supply of meds, my mobile phone, face masks, hand sanitizer, anti-bac wipes, and a pair of rubber gloves. I quickly add a large flask of sweet tea, four plastic mugs, and a family-size pack of chocolate digestives. Grabbing the house and car keys off the hook in the utility room, I do a quick check around and lock the door.

Sadie, my reliable mini minor and I are at the bank. Using my blue badge I pull into a parking spot, right outside. I keep the engine running, hop out, and open the two doors and the boot. I adjust the two front seats so passengers can get in the back. Standing at the open driver's door I check my watch, 1.00 pm. Up to this point, I had functioned on adrenaline. Now, I've got a massive attack of the collywobbles. My heart pounding, I want to slam the doors shut and drive back to my quiet, safe life. I also feel stimulated, excited, and more alive than I have in a long time. Reaching into the holdall in the driver's footwell, I pull out a face mask, put it on, and sanitize my fidgeting hands. Alarms ring and lights flash, three men in balaclavas run straight past me. "Excuse me, I'm your driver," I shout.

"What the—"

"Where's Alfie? Where's the red Jag we nicked for the job?"

"Who the bleeding hell is Super Gran here?"

"Get in," ordered the voice I recognised from the phone call. I'd christened him, The Boss.

His two, 6'-6" hunky accomplices threw the bags they were carrying into Sadie's boot. Clashing heads and bickering they squeezed in, knees under their chins, bodies bent double. Readjusting the front seats, I got in. The Boss deposited his bag, slammed the boot shut, and jumped into the passenger seat. "Drive, Lady, drive," he ordered.

15

"Seat belts please, boys. Here, take a face mask and a squirt of sanitizer. Can't be too careful."

"Please, Lady, drive, drive, drive," begged The Boss.

Sadie responded and we were away.

"Faster, faster, Lady. Put your foot down."

"I'm observing the speed limit, 30 miles per hour in town. I closed my ears to the bad language, put my foot down and asked The Boss, "Where do you want me to drive to?"

"Head for the motorway."

Sadie crept gradually up to 80 miles per hour, bless her. It wasn't easy for her to carry all that weight. I hadn't driven that fast in years, it was exhilarating. Noticing the sign, 'Last petrol before motorway', I broke fast and pulled onto the garage forecourt.

"What the f***?" questioned all three men at once.

"I need petrol if we are going out of town."

The Boss shouted, "Out, out, out." He jumped into the driver's seat of a black BMW X7 SUV, which was stupidly left ticking over while its owner went to pay. Sadie's boot contents were stashed in the BMW.

"That's more like it, speed and power," announced one of the hunks.

"What about Super Gran, Boss?" shouted the other.

"Shove her in the back, move it."

Bundled in and jolted forward as The Boss shot off, it took me a minute or two to get settled. I like sitting up high, overlooking the traffic. Very plush and comfy. Lots of legroom. I must have a word with those two hunks and tell them to be gentle with me. I knew them from somewhere, got it! 'The Sky Twins', Rosie's grandsons, Will and Ben. Rosie Sky is my bridge partner at the retirement village. I changed my glasses, pulled out the flask, and asked, "Does anyone fancy a nice cup of tea?

"Super Gran's nodded off. What are we gonna do about her, Boss?"

"I don't know, Will. We've got to follow the plan through now."

"And it doesn't include her," insisted Will.

"The old lady must need a pee. The services are coming up, Boss, why don't we let her go into the building, then drive off? She'll be safe there," suggested Ben.

"Super Gran, a chance to use the loo, you better go. Don't know when we'll be able to stop again." Ben tried his plan.

"Oh, goodness, I dropped off."

"Off you go, meet back here in five. You take care now," persisted Ben.

"I'm OK, I never go much in the day."

"Takeaway tea or a sandwich?" coaxed Will.

"We had tea and biscuits earlier. That will see me through to dinner time."

"Stretch your legs?" tried Ben.

"I'll sit here and wait, thanks love."

The Boss pulled off again, shaking his head. Will slammed his hand hard on the door panel, "It's 13.30, Boss."

"Right, lads, I'm taking the next junction off - the cops have probably picked us up on the motorway cameras. Read out the B-road route to the farm, Ben. We'll swap cars and re-join the motorway at junction 25, from there it's ten minutes to the airfield. The jet is scheduled to leave at 14.30."

"You can't fly, Boris won't let you," I said.

"Won't let you rob banks neither, but that didn't stop us," sniggered Will.

"I didn't pack my passport."

"What makes you think you're coming?" Will questioned.

"I can't go home. I will have been identified on the cameras outside the bank."

"Should have thought about that before you got involved," responded Will.

"I didn't think beyond doing something exciting." My chest tightened and I struggled to breathe. I realized I'd outlived my usefulness. "I need my medication."

"What's the tablets for Super Gran?" questioned Ben as he rummaged in my holdall.

"Dicky ticker." Feeling physically and mentally exhausted I closed my eyes and had a quiet chat with Sid.

"She's nodded off again. Ring Alfie. Get him to collect her from the airfield," suggested Will.

"It's bitter out there, Will. And If I were Alfie, I'd stay well away from The Boss."

"You're too bloody soft, Ben, always have been."

"What if Super Gran were Granny Rosie?"

"She ain't, is she?"

"I could be," I joined in, innocently.

"What do you mean, you could be?" questioned Will suspiciously.

"Rosie Sky would be so disappointed in you boys."

"She knows who we are." There was fear in Will's voice.

Sid had suggested I tell them I knew who they were, he said it would buy me time. For the moment I held a little power over them. It would go one way or the other now. They would take me with them or get rid of me. They didn't have much time to decide.

The door opened slowly, and a line of silver light shone across the floor, illuminating our way down the aisle of the luxury jet. The interior was about four feet high by five feet wide. There were four large, soft leather seats, one behind the other. A steward in a smart black and maroon uniform welcomed us aboard, seated us, and handed each of us a large whisky with ice in cut glass tumblers.

"Good evening, madame, gentlemen. My name is Charles and your pilot's name is Adam. It is our pleasure to take care of you on this seven-hour flight to Bahrain. Please fasten your seat belts and put your seats in the upright position. We will be taking off immediately." Handing us the usual flight safety jargon, he went on, "For your comfort, we have bathrooms, a food galley, and an inflight entertainment menu. I will serve a hot meal in one hour, allowing you ample time to shower, change, and relax with a pre-meal drink. If you require anything, please do not hesitate to ask."

Bahrain, the Middle East, Persian Gulf. I will never see Blighty again. I checked my wristwatch, 7.30 pm.

"Do you require anything, madam?"

"No thank you, Charles. And please call me Gertie."

He tapped the right-hand side of his nose with his forefinger and winked at me. "We don't use your names, madame."

"Sorry!"

18

"Could I bring you a blanket and pillow? Your seat reclines to a sleeping position. There are still two hours before we land."

"That sounds perfect. Could I have a glass of water to take a tablet, please? And Charles, I would like something."

"Madame?"

"Another large whisky." I sipped the whisky and did my best to relax. I heard The Boss tell Charles to leave the bottle. Then I heard him chuckle to himself.

"Our lady's gone to sleep again. It took guts to do what she did today. We'd have been in the soup if she hadn't been outside the bank." He chuckled again and did an impression of me, "Excuse me, I'm your driver."

Ben smiled. "Does anyone fancy a nice cup of tea?"

"She's priceless, lads."

"What she is, is a problem, Boss," persisted Will.

"I'm not sure she is, Will. As I see it, she did Alfie's job, she's entitled to his cut."

"Hang on, Boss."

"No, you hang on, Will, The Boss is right. She saved us today."

"She knows who we are, Ben."

"She ain't gonna shop us, she's in this up to her neck."

I woke and instinctively checked my wristwatch again. 8.30 pm, one hour before we'd land. I looked around the cabin, The Boss and Will were napping. Ben was reading a magazine about motorbikes. Bringing my seat into the upright position, I disturbed him.

"Hi there, Super Gran. Do you feel better for your sleep?"

"No, not really Ben, I'm terrified."

"Don't be, trust us to look after you."

"Can I ask you a few questions?"

"Fire away, you're one of us now."

"What did you, we, steal?"

"Documents, that we'll exchange with a wealthy bloke in Bahrain for lots of money. That's all we know. We stole an envelope from a safety deposit box, and we're not allowed to open it."

"What's in all those bags then?"

"We figured we might as well withdraw some cash while we were there!"

"How did you get in the vault, the safety deposit box?"

"Same old story. We held the bank manager's family hostage. He was putty."

"Why Bahrain?"

"No extradition treaty with the UK. Just a little added precaution. After a while, we can go where we want."

"Not home."

"No, not home."

"You will miss your family, your gran."

"We started out as petty thieves and look at us now, bank robbers. The gangs, the drug lords, the criminal families on the estates, it's not a nice place to live. Our family doesn't know any of the details, but they know it's one last job, it's our way out of this life. We're going to start over. If we don't get out now, we'll end up dead or banged up for life."

"Your gran will miss you."

"She will at first. She's been diagnosed with dementia and she's deteriorating fast. We've organized for money to be available for the best care she can get."

"That explains some of the bridge hands she's played lately," I chuckled.

Charles entered the cabin and woke The Boss and Will. "Landing in twenty minutes, would you please fasten your seatbelts and put your seats in the upright position. It just remains for me to say, enjoy Bahrain."

As the jet dropped smoothly, my heart started pounding. I was aware of blood pumping loudly through my ears, thump, thump, my vision blurred, chest pain, tingling, couldn't breathe, blackness.

I open my eyes. I'm in a large, cool room. *Better lay still and see how I feel. I'm not sure what happened to me.*

"Ah, you awake." A young lady who I assume is from Bahrain hovers over me.

"How you feel?"

"I don't know. I'm scared to move."

"You can move."

I still lie there, not daring to try. "Have I had a heart attack?" I ask, afraid of the answer.

"No. You had panic attack. Same symptoms sometimes."

"A panic attack, now I feel silly."

"Panic attacks very common. You have a stressful day, no?

"Yes, very stressful."

While we are talking, she takes my pulse and temperature, moves my limbs, and runs a finger in front of my eyes.

"You fine, Lady. Sit up now and I bring doctor and English tea."

A very handsome young man in a smart suit enters the room. "Good afternoon, madame. How do you feel?"

"Silly. All this fuss over a panic attack."

"Your friends insisted you were thoroughly examined."

"My friends?"

"Yes, the gentlemen you arrived with. You are perfectly well. I took the liberty of going through your bag and found a copy of a prescription in your purse. Heart tablets, blood pressure tablets, water tablets, antacid for the stomach. Plus, a medication for pain. Is this for arthritis?"

I nod my head.

"I have given you a new supply of everything and I can continue to supply them."

"How much do I owe you, Doctor? And how much will it cost to supply these tablets ongoing," I ask, worrying how I'm going to finance this. I don't think Bahrain has NHS.

"That has all been taken care of by your friends. You can get up after your tea. Take it steady, and take care of the heat, you need to adjust to it gradually. I will leave my card. Goodbye, madame."

Someone has kindly laid out a selection of clothes and shoes in my size. I choose a beautiful pale blue kaftan and sandals. There are toiletries, sun cream, mossy stuff, a large straw hat, sunglasses, and a cotton shawl. I bathe and dress. The young lady keeps checking on me.

"Look under your pillow," she says, smiling at me.

Under my pillow is a photo of Sid I carry in my purse; he is with me all the time. The Boss comes in and gives me a bear hug.

21

"You gave us a right fright, Lady. We thought you were having a heart attack."

"Only a panic attack, it seems," I reply.

"Thank God."

"Do you mean that, Boss?" I ask cautiously.

"Of course, I do. I've grown fond of you."

"What about Will?"

"He's not a bad lad. He might have left you for Alfie to collect but he wouldn't want any harm to come to you."

The Boss opens a patio door onto a terrace. A young man is setting out bread, local cheese and iced water with lemon. We sit at the table, and I realize I am very hungry.

"Have some food while I fill you in on what's happened. We were driven to this villa from the plane. It's ours for as long as we want to stay. You'll love it, it's beautiful, got everything, servants, swimming pool, air-con, you name it, it's got it. The bloke we did the robbery for was here when we arrived. Flew in by helicopter, he never spoke a word, I've no idea where he's from." He checked the contents of the envelope. Once he was happy, he had his assistant issue us passports, visas, and bank statements in our new names. Our cuts for doing the job and the value of all the stuff we nicked from the bank have been converted into dinar and put in the accounts. He wrote the value in pounds under the dinar figure. Here are your documents."

He places a passport and a bank statement on the table. I stare at him and the documents. I open the passport, the name inside is Gertrude Shaw. I'm Gertrude Evans. Tentatively, I read the bank statement. My heart starts pounding, I can hear the blood pulsing through my ears, my vision blurs, I can't breathe, blackness.

"Lady, lady, bloody hell, she's done it again!"

I come around very quickly.

"Will you stop doing that?"

"Sorry, Boss, it was the shock, all that money."

"It's your cut. We couldn't have done it without you and, as you said, you can't go home." He hands me a brown paper bag. "Breathe into this, it will help calm your breathing down."

"How you doing, Super Gran?" asked Ben from the patio doors. I could see Will was right behind him.

"I'm in shock."

"Boss has given you the good news, then? You're famous at home, Super Gran, or should I call you, The Golden Oldie, or Geriatric Gertie, or, my personal favorite, The Old Lady of Cotswold's Street. Like the Old Lady of Threadneedle Street." He laughs and spreads British newspapers on the table - all with a picture of me outside the bank and all giving me a catchy name in the headline.

"Goodness," I exclaim. I turn and study Will. "Are you ok with me having this money and being here?" I ask.

"It's taken me a while, I realize now you're in the same position as us, you're no danger to me. You did the getaway drivers' job, so you deserve the cut. The one thing that puzzles me is who is Alfie to you?"

"I don't know Alfie."

"Is he your grandson?"

"I never had children."

"You don't have to protect him. We won't hurt him. You must know Alfie; he's the only other person who knew The Boss's burner phone number."

"What phone?"

"The number you rang me on, Gertie," explains The Boss, finally using my Christian name.

"I got it out the phone book."

"It's not in the phone book, Gertie, it's a mobile."

"Ben, would you fetch my phone from the table in my room please," I requested.

The Boss studies the mobile, the burner phone number is the last number rung. "I think I know what you did Gertie. I think you misdialed; the local code is 01739, you dialed 07739."

I burst into uncontrollable laughter. All this came about because I dialed the wrong number!

EPILOGUE

I've been living in Bahrain for 10 months. I love the sun; the heat's great for my arthritis. I have to wear trousers and long skirts and cover my head and arms sometimes, but I don't mind that. I love wandering the mazes of the souk, seeing all the brightly coloured spices and breathing in their aromas, mixed with those of coffee and sugary sweets. I love the Bollywood films at the cinema. The beaches are amazing, with white pearl sands. The shopping malls are out of this world. I've been dolphin-watching, visited mosques and forts, and learned a lot about the history of the place. I am learning to play golf at the moment.

People from all over the world work here. But a foreign lady doesn't wander around alone. I have a driver who accompanies me everywhere. His name is Aharon, and he is a knowledgeable companion. The local people are very nice to me. There are private beaches and hotels where I can meet English holidaymakers. I've learned a little Arabic - I'm finding that hard going. Mostly, I'm very happy but I miss a good gossip. Boss, Will, and Ben are still here, soon they will move on. I have been thinking about my future. I think it would be a good idea to bring Rosie Sky out here. Money can buy most things, as I know from experience, getting her here without anyone knowing where she went would be no problem. Rosie and I always got along well. I'm sure seeing the twins, the sun, the colours, aromas, beautiful views, and dips in the warm sea would stimulate and benefit her in the good times left to her. I know it would benefit me to see her. When the time comes, I can keep an eye and make sure she has the best care. After that, who knows?

THE END

Note: During the Covid lockdown, Grimsby Writers held their meetings on Zoom. The above story came about from members setting three lines to inspire the beginning, middle, and end of a story. The lines were: -

During the pandemic, a lonely woman calls a random number and arranges a blind meet-up.

Last petrol before motorway.

The door opened slowly, and a line of light shone across the floor.

1994 – Pulp Fiction (Quentin Tarantino) hit the cinemas.

The 30 Day Warning

Alan Gilbert

Jeremy was upstairs when he noticed the postman walking away from the house.

'It's about time,' he said to himself, 'that book should have been here two days ago.' Before he even reached the bottom of the stairs, Jeremy could see that there was no parcel, a shiver shot down his spine. 'Don't be silly,' he reassured himself, 'many people use small blue envelopes.' As Jeremy picked it up, he could see the distinctive well-rounded writing. He knew it well, even the colour of the ink was that used by his wife in her beloved fountain pen, but Marianne had been dead for nearly a year. Jeremy dropped the letter. He needed a drink. After a small Glenhobley, Jeremy opened the envelope and began to read.

Dear Jeremy,

You will of course realise that thirty days from now will be the first anniversary of my unfortunate death. We spent our last night together at the Lugger Inn in Pauldeen and if you book the same room for the night, I will find a way to talk to you. You may or may not realise *that Aunt Sarah has recently died and despite being adopted, I am her sole heir without my help, you will not be able to access her, not inconsiderable, estate.*

Your loving wife,
Marianne

Should he call the police? There was no doubt in Jeremy's mind that his wife was dead. Although her body had been in the sea for two weeks and battered by rocks, she was wearing the right clothes and jewellery. DNA confirmation, though, was impossible since her real parents could not be traced. Jeremy needed another drink.

A couple of hours later, a troubled Jeremy sat on the floor with his fourth whisky of the day. Startled when the telephone rang, he hauled himself from the floor, reached for the handset, and spilled the remaining liquid. He seemed unable to even touch the instrument. He began to shake. Marianne had organised the landline as part of a broadband deal but, for many months now, there had been no callers.

'Probably just a wrong number,' he reassured himself and decided on an early night.

The next few days were uneventful and Jeremy pushed the letter to the back of his mind. But one evening, as he walked into the house, the telephone was ringing. This time he picked it up.

'Is that Mr Cartley, Mr Jeremy Cartley?'

'Er... no,' replied a startled Jeremy.

'Well, this is Sergeant Wilkinson of the Devon and Cornwall Police. Could you please ask him to contact me as soon as possible?'

'Er... yes,' answered a terrified Jeremy. He could have admitted who he was. He would then have known what the call was about. But he hadn't and was completely in the dark. Since his wife's death, Jeremy had become quite isolated. He hadn't realised that everyone they knew were Marianne's friends and since the funeral, he had heard nothing from them. Even Margaret, of all people, had abandoned him after a few emails. A couple of drinks would calm him down he decided.

When Jeremy arrived home the following evening, he discovered another blue envelope with the same writing and ink. He opened it immediately.

Dear Jeremy,

Since you haven't yet booked our room at the Lugger, I have done it for you. It is an important anniversary after all. The following morning you can visit the beautiful spot where I fell. We will be able to talk there. Remember, someone must claim Aunt Sarah's estate.

Your loving wife,
Marianne

Jeremy reassured himself that he would have needed a glass of Glenhobley even without the arrival of the letter. It was a much calmer man who sat down and thought through the situation. Ghosts do not exist. Even if they did, he reasoned, they couldn't possibly be capable of sticking a stamp on an envelope. So whoever was responsible for the letters must be a cruel joker. Jeremy knew that Aunt Sarah had indeed died so someone was interested in her estate. This person wanted something and blackmail had to be involved. Whoever it was had to be dealt with and he or she couldn't possibly know that Jeremy had a revolver. An illegal weapon of course but that didn't matter. He would make the journey to Cornwall and confront this wretched individual.

There were no more letters but the telephone rang several times only to be ignored by Jeremy. When the day arrived, he was packed and ready. On the journey to Cornwall, his mood changed from one of fear to one of eager anticipation. He felt prepared for anything. On arriving at the Lugger, Jeremy noticed that there was something a little different about the inn. He stood and stared for a short while. The sign featuring the sailing vessel looked new. In fact, the windows had all been painted and the masonry itself appeared fresh. He went inside.

The bar, he observed, had been transformed. The tables and chairs were all dark-coloured oak and the bar looked far brighter, yet remained authentic. The barmaid caught his eye. 'Can I help you sir?'

'I think I may have a room booked but I'm not quite sure.'

'Can you come to the end of the bar?' Once there, the barmaid opened up a book.

'What was the name please?'

'Cartley, Jeremy Cartley.'

'Oh, yes! There it is.'

'Do you know who booked the room,' asked Jeremy.

'Well, that's the funny thing. We don't have a website and all of our bookings are made over the phone. There are three of us who deal with booking rooms and we always write in this book in pencil,' she said tapping a large book on the counter. None of us recognize the writing for your room and it's written in ink.'

She then spun the book around and pointed to an entry. Jeremy's legs began to weaken.

'Are you all right, sir?' she asked and a concerned customer leapt towards Jeremy and led him to a chair.

A short while later Jeremy was sitting in his bedroom. He had seen a good likeness of Marianne's writing. It couldn't be real because she was dead.

'Ghosts do not exist,' he told himself. 'When I find this joker, he will be very sorry.' He stood up, walked to his suitcase, opened it, and pulled out the old revolver. He then moved a couple of pillows, sat in the centre of the bed, and leaned back, still holding the weapon. Jeremy drifted into sleep.

A short while later, Jeremy was awake and staring at the wall. For a few seconds, he was back at home, facing the Cornish harbour scene on the wall directly in front of him. The same framed print could be found on his bedroom wall. He looked around the room. Since his last visit it had been re-decorated and the furniture was all new, but there was something odd about it. 'I'm just tired and hungry,' Jeremy decided.

Later in the evening, Jeremy walked into the bar and immediately caught the barman's eye.

'Good evening, sir, what can I get you?'

'I don't suppose you have a Glenhobley.'

'Of course, I rarely drink anything else, it's one advantage of being the landlord, I'm Bernie by the way.' Jeremy introduced himself and over the next couple of hours discovered that Bernie had owned the Lugger for twelve years. His wife, however, had left after eight of them. 'I didn't blame her because it's a long day and very hard to get any time away.'

Back in his room, Jeremy found it difficult to sleep and was shaved and showered by 6 a.m. There was no night porter, so he slipped out of the inn and went for a walk. He couldn't quite face up to the coastal path just yet and so wandered around the almost deserted small town. On returning to the Lugger he went to his bedroom and waited.

Jeremy emerged from the inn just before 7.30 a.m., reasoning that it should take about twenty minutes to reach the place. He patted his pocket to confirm that the revolver was present and began to walk up the hill towards the coastal path. Quite soon he could see an overhanging rock. The place he wanted was just beyond this. Then he noticed someone sitting on a bench drinking from a small silver cup and staring out to sea. It was Bernie.

Bernie smiled at him. 'Good morning Jeremy. Admiring the view from here sets me up for the day. My wife could never understand though.'

'No, they never understand,' replied Jeremy.

'Fancy a drop?'

'Why not,' replied Jeremy, happy to delay the meeting. 'What are you drinking?'

'Glenhobley.'

Jeremy eagerly swallowed the offered liquid. This was a good omen. Bernie poured a second and offered it to Jeremy.

'Are you sure?'

'Of course, but I'll put it on your bill, laughed Bernie. Jeremy quickly disposed of the second drink.

'Anyway, I had better get back and do some work. Have a good day.' With that, Bernie stood up and began walking down the hill toward the town.

'Right. There is no point in putting it off any longer,' said Jeremy, to no one in particular and once again began climbing the hill.

As he neared his goal, Jeremy's legs began to ache. 'I will have to join a gymnasium when this is all over,' he mumbled. As he drew level with the secluded spot, Jeremy gasped. Seated, looking out to sea was a woman, wearing the same clothes as his wife. Despite having her back to him, she spoke. 'Why don't you join me, Jeremy?' It was his wife's voice and when she turned to face him, he fell to his knees. There could be no doubt, it *was* his wife and Jeremy seemed unable to move.

'There's plenty of room on the bench,' said his wife. The woman stood up and walked towards him. 'Let me help you up,' she said, pushing her hands under his armpits and hauling him from the ground. With Jeremy leaning against her, the woman moved to the bench and lowered him into a sitting position. The confused and terrified man was incapable of sitting upright without her support.

'I had been reading your emails for months,' she began.' and was well aware of you and Margaret's plan to kill me. The chance meeting in the cafe, the suggestion that she and I should take an early morning walk up here where you would be waiting to push me into the water. However, I used my medical knowledge to alter your plan. You and I were awake early that morning. I got out of bed and made you a coffee. The drink included a crushed sleeping pill and quite quickly, you fell asleep. This allowed Margaret and I to leisurely walk up to this beautiful spot.

'Your mistress was enjoying the view as she waited for you to appear but was rather surprised when I stuck a hypodermic in her neck. The effect was almost instantaneous and she fell to the ground paralysed. You will have realized by now that the oral version takes a little longer but is just as effective.' Jeremy was making frantic little movements with his arms by now. His wife gave him a big smile and continued.

'It took me a while to exchange our clothes and I had to keep checking that no one was near us. You were so late that I had to give her another injection, but when you finally arrived you saw a woman leaning on a rock looking out to sea. You didn't speak or confirm that it was me; you just pushed the poor woman over the edge. You looked round wondering where Margaret was but, at the sound of people approaching, you just fled.

'I can see the terror in your eyes now, Jeremy but let's look through your pockets.' Already wearing gloves, Marianne pulled the revolver out of a pocket. 'Were you planning to kill me twice Jeremy? I think this can stay with you but my two letters must disappear. In case you are wondering how I survived, I just took over Margaret's identity. Since she had friends it took a lot of work but isn't internet banking wonderful? Particularly when someone keeps a nice notebook containing all the account numbers and passwords. She was quite wealthy. I can see why she was so attractive.'

Jeremy was conscious that someone was now standing beside him. He began to have hope until Marianne spoke. 'You have already met Bernie, haven't you? He and I have great plans for the Lugger. I'm surprised you didn't notice my design flair in the bedroom. I have recently reappeared as myself recovering from amnesia. The police thought I was a fake and tried to contact you but since you failed to respond we switched to plan B.

Jeremy found himself being lifted by two people over the fence in front of the bench.

'Right Jeremy, you are now going to have your first flying lesson. Don't worry, it's only a short course and I won't be asking any questions at the end.

1994 - The Channel Tunnel was opened to the public, linking England and France.

For Thirty Years I've Trod the Path

Ian Walker

The special day has started,
I realised when I woke,
If only I'd departed,
I'd avoid the annual joke,
Of celebrating my long life,
I've lived another year,
Another year without my wife,
I wish that she were near.

But now I've lived 100 years,
To some a milestone,
To me it only brings the tears,
Because I live alone.
A telegram from royalty,
And Birthday Cards galore,
To me it's just insanity,
'cause life is just a bore.

They say that I am fortunate,
To live a life so long,
For me it's just a time to wait,
Until the angel's song.
Elisa died at sixty-seven,
Too young to leave my side,
And now she waits for me in heaven,
I can't wait for that ride.

For thirty years I've trod the path,
Of widower and parent,
I can't wait 'til I hear her laugh,
And talk of times we spent,
Together we lived a life so full,
She was my true soulmate,
But then life turned from bright to dull,
And now I have to wait.

It's time to wash and clothe myself,
The crowd will soon arrive,
To raise a drink up for my health,
Because I'm still alive.
To be of healthy mind and heart,
It leads to so much praise,
But there's no effort on my part,
To live so many days.

It's all to do with DNA,
They say I have good genes,
I wish that they'd just go away,
And leave me to my means.
When the joyfulness has passed,
The party-goers gone,
I pray to God – don't let me last,
To one-hundred-and-one.

January 1994 - After two years of talks between Ukraine, Russia and America, Ukraine agreed to get rid of its nuclear weapons if Russia would respect its sovereignty.

Starfighters

Denise Light

Stephen looked at his watch. Still plenty of time. On his way to catch the latest shuttle to Moonbase Two, he couldn't quite believe that after all this time he had got the job. It had always been his wish to go to the moon but without the requisite quality of exam results, he learned early on that this was just a pipe dream. So, he went to university and studied engineering. And he found he was quite good. He was good at designing, good at diagnosing faults, and even better at putting stuff together in perfect working order.

It hadn't taken Stephen long to get hired by one of the biggest engineering firms. Having started in the industry, it wasn't long before he was transferred to the aerospace division. He was a perfectionist, and it became obvious to his bosses that he was a huge asset.

Obviously, all the space-going vehicles needed to have no faults—no design faults, and particularly no faults with the components. People's lives depended on them to be perfect. In his early days working on the rockets, Stephen had had altercations with some of the suppliers who he felt were making substandard parts.

In the early days of the Moonbases, the space vehicles were not as reliable as they should have been, and key people had been lost. At the time it was felt that this was expected and people had to take their chances.

When Stephen was transferred to the aerospace section, he was put in charge of the inner linings of the space vehicles, all the rockets, the little spaceships, and the defensive/attack vehicles. These had to be airtight, and Stephen concentrated on making the inside of all the vehicles as safe as possible. In one year, the number of space personnel lost to lining failure was reduced to nearly zero. Although the improved quality of the linings meant that they were costing more, there were no lives lost which meant no compensation had to be paid to the families.

For the next few years, Stephen moved from one section to another making sure that everything was done to the highest specification. Not only did this mean that they were losing fewer people, but they were also able to improve their whole space program and increase the number of Moonbases. More people were using the Moon as a jumping-off point to explore other worlds and as a result, other countries were getting interested in space exploration and what advantages it would bring them.

Inevitably there were conflicts. The aerospace industry had inevitably changed to producing Starfighters which were small and manoeuvrable and designed for combat in the atmosphere or space. Stephen had been involved in the initial designs but as time went on, he had to think of new and better space fighters. There were not enough hours in the day for Stephen to do everything he wanted. He had learned to delegate after he had an initial idea. His team was excellent, and the Moonbases had been supplied with a good supply of Starfighters and other space vehicles.

One day Stephen's CEO sent for him. This was nothing new to Stephen for he and his boss had often met to discuss Stephen's plans as well as the state of their part of the industry. But today Stephen was shocked to find what was planned for him.

He was to go to the Moon. Specifically, to Moonbase Two which was where many of the Starfighters were based. As things were, there were now many Starfighters and many pilots on the moonbases but very few engineers so when things went wrong, and they inevitably did, there were not the experts to put the fighters back together.

So here he was. Ready to fulfil his lifelong dream of going to the Moon. The Shuttle was there on the launch pad and Stephen joined the other engineers. They were going to be his team. Many of them he already knew. Some he had recommended; some he only knew by reputation. But like him, they had never been in space before and there were some nerves. Again, like him, they were mostly excited.

The Shuttle took the engineers straight to Moonbase Two. On arrival, they were shown to their quarters and given a day to acclimatise. Stephen used his time wisely. He checked out his team and made sure that each person was looking forward to their job.

The next day they were taken to the part of the base where the Starfighters were stored. A large space, Stephen could hardly believe his eyes when he saw just how many of the small fighters there were. He was told that lots of them needed work doing, so the first thing he did was to get organised. The team checked each fighter in turn. Out of the fifty, there were sixteen that needed a great deal of work just to get them back in the air. There were twenty with minor problems, so Stephen assigned two of his team to work on those while he and the rest of them concentrated on the ones that needed the most work.

Day after day they worked on the Starfighters. On the twentieth day, Stephen gave his team a small celebration because they had virtually finished their repairs and most of the Starfighters were now fit to fly.

While Stephen had been on the Moon, things had not been going on so well politically. Other countries had started attacking Moonbase One. They felt that they should be involved in space exploration on an equal basis and were prepared to fight to get their way. One country had been arming their own pilots with their own version of the Starfighters and had become quite aggressive. It had got so bad that one day Stephen had seen ten Starfighters take off from Moonbase Two to get the foreigners to leave. One thing led to another and only nine Starfighters had returned to base. The tenth had been blown up by the aggressor. So, there was only one thing to do. *Fight*!

Stephen and his engineers were kept busy. But this elite team meant that Moonbase Two was kept fully armed with Starfighters.

Then came the day to end all days. Moonbase Two had forty-nine Starfighters, all working, and that day thirty of them set off to try and force the intruders to leave completely. Stephen stayed at the base ready for the fighters to return. As he sat there looking out at the stars he thought back to when his ancestors were waiting for planes to come back from bombing Germany during the Second World War. A hundred years later, and he was doing the same thing, just waiting for the Starfighters to return. Fifty odd years ago had been the Falklands War, like this one it hadn't lasted long. And like this one there had been people watching the planes as they left and then waiting for them to return in one piece. Stephen stayed where he was, watching and waiting for the Starfighters to return.

And return they did. They came zooming in, one, two, three, four.... he could hardly keep up with them.....fifteen, sixteen..... twenty-eight, twenty-nine......thirty. He had counted them all out and he had counted them all back!

1994 – After years of Apartheid, South Africa saw its first black President take office when Nelson Mandela was sworn in.

When I was 30

Pauline Murdoch

In 1964, my husband Bill, was posted to a mission hospital in Tanzania. We had already spent 2 ½ years in Batlharos mission, in the Kalahari Desert area of Northern Cape Province, South Africa. We had three children Susan aged five, Janet 3, and John 18 months. On my 30th birthday, it came time to move on from Bill's job as the sole doctor in charge of (180 bedded) St Michaels Mission Hospital in Batlharos, to work for Bishop Trevor Huddleston in the hospital in Masasi, Tanganyika (just United with Zanzibar, now Tanzania.)

A MEMORABLE JOURNEY

We had an interesting journey getting to Masasi. The following section is what I recorded in my diary. We were travelling from Batlharos, near Kuruman, Republic of South Africa to a new workplace in the newly independent and newly united Republic of Tanganyika and Zanzibar or Tanzania. There was my husband Bill, three children aged 5, 3, and 18 months and myself. We began by travelling from the mission in Kalahari down to Kimberley, where we had recently bought an old Volkswagen Combi which we loaded up with our belongings. We set off on our journey, heading for the first stop in Johannesburg.

Unfortunately, after about 30 miles it gave up the ghost and ground to a noisy halt. We were lucky. The hospital maintenance man, Edward Moorcroft came to our rescue. "A cracked broken chassis." He pronounced, and proceeded to wire it together "to hold up the engine awhile." We were able to drive 120 miles to Kimberley and the garage where it was bought and got our money back.

We eventually made our way to Jane Furse Hospital in the Transkei, where we spent several weeks.

1964: September 21 Jane Furse Mission

Bill is getting valuable experience in a Mission Hospital large enough to employ eight doctors of various specialities, and running numerous district clinics among the mainly *Pedi* people, who speak a language closely related to Tswana. We shall then proceed on our journey to Masasi in Tanzania. We now have a passage booked on the SS *Braemar Castle* leaving from Lourenco Marques in Moçambique.

December 8, Salvation Army Hostel- Dar es Salaam

Our last evening in South Africa, we spent in a small guest house near the railway which will take us across the frontier and onto the docks in L.M. We had taken our luggage to the station, more than 20 heavy cases in boxes with all our household effects. The children had five hours to sleep, with the landlord ready to wake us at midnight to catch the 1 am train.

Suddenly I heard my husband call, "Wake up, wake up, it's 2 am!" You can imagine the panic we felt as we gathered together our belongings and three sleepy children. There might not be another train for several days and we could miss our sailing. The landlord shared our panic and offered his taxi to the station. The taxi refused to start!
As the minutes ticked by we reflected how certain it was we had missed the train. The very penitent landlord offered the van in which he collected his coal. We all sat on the black and dusty floor, being shaken dirtier with every bump.

When we reached the station, we were amazed and more than relieved to see our train just arriving. Our luggage is safely locked away in a shed. Bill, rushed to repossess it, but the shed was firmly locked and we did not know who had the key. The only porter was busy at the far end of the second long train between our platform and the luggage shed.

Our very long train was the overnight kind with births. Fortunately for us, there seems no hurry although the train is running more than two hours late. I was able to settle the children down to sleep, anxiously peering out of the windows from time to time to see if Bill was coming with the cases. The train began to splutter into life making hissing and puffing noises. Out there eventually the key was found, but no help was offered. To get the items onto our train they had to be carried, one or two at a time, onto the other train at the 1st platform and out the other side to reach our trains guard's van,

I didn't know whether to go and help. Leave the children on the train which could whisk them away at any moment, or stay put. Panic! What if we went off without Bill, who had the tickets, the visas, all the money, the passports, and *everything*? After what seems a very long time (it was!) Bill appeared smiling with the last two heavy cases, just as our train started slowly to move. He managed to wrestle open the door of the van, throw in the cases, and climb aboard. With sighs of relief, we awaited him negotiating the corridors; so we set off on our journey towards the Portuguese Frontier. Just eighteen stops to Lourenco Marques. But what would the third *frontier* stop have been like, at 3:30 am *if Bill had been left behind* with the last two items of luggage, and all our documents?

Our journey then became a delightful holiday. The Portuguese customs man recommended *Pensao Estoril* for the four nights until we sailed. A large guest house on the main Avenue with scarlet, flamboyant trees currently in full bloom welcoming us. The proprietor was a motherly woman who took our children to her heart. The varied clientele included a retired sailor who had chosen this house in this country, from all the world that he had travelled, for his final retirement home. We could see exactly why, L.M. was a beautiful seaside town as well as a Port city. We were sad to leave it so soon, but then it was also thrilling to board our second Union Castle Liner for the journey up the East Coast. A bit smaller, but every bit as comfortable as in the Athlone Castle. We had an extra treat. Three days and nights of hotel food and care, we stopped in BEIRA harbour whilst the hold of the ship was loaded with bars of copper. The cranes were swinging them aboard as fast as possible throughout the 24-hour, days without pause until we departed. Meantime, we could explore Beira, home of the giant prawns, and a seaside playground for settlers from the Rhodesias. Next stop Dar es Salaam.

We woke early peering out of the port hole - at a claimant for the title of the most beautiful natural harbour in the World. We were met by a priest who took us to a Salvation Army Hostel. This is a delightful area of gardens with shady coconut palm trees. There are many chalets thatched with palm leaves, including a veranda. There is a large restaurant for the guests; we are very comfortable and central to explore the town. Again, a pleasant city with docks and beaches; and here Arabic and German influences are everywhere and it is sunny and hot. Bill flew to Masasi to meet Bishop Trevor Huddleston, and Eric Williams the departing doctor. He was held up at gunpoint by a TANU youth patrol who were checking tax certificates. His priest escort in the car explained that the passport meant he was not yet resident and all was well. The hospital has no kitchen, and relatives camp around the ward to feed the patients in their beds. Now he has returned and is arranging a flight to take us with luggage south to Mkomaindo Hospital, Masasi.

December 12th Mkomaindo,

We have all arrived safely at Mkomaindo Mission in Masasi, Mtwara Region. Our home is a typical colonial-style house with a large veranda to keep the rooms cool. I was amazed to see the windows had no glass, only mosquito netting. What do I do I wondered when it gets cold at night. I was forgetting, we are now in the tropics!

We are in a civil servant's house a little away from the hospital, and unlike the mission accommodation we have running water, but no one has gas or electricity. The bathroom is indoors and we have a shower which the children think is fabulous. The rooms in the house are large and airy with high ceilings. The large bedroom has three cots in it for our three children. The sitting room is a very large room with plenty of space for visitors. Our neighbour is the Chief of Police, from a tribe in the North. We are surrounded by Yao and Makua people speaking two of the 100 tribal languages of Tanganyika. Our neighbour's children speak another. Adults are all expected to speak Swahili. Children must speak and learn Swahili in school. Already ahead of us, our children have learned some Swahili which they sing and chant with delight.

East African people are very different from the friends we left behind in Northern Cape. They are quieter, but more colourful. A woman will plait her hair and wear a kanga (a brightly printed, light, African cotton cloth, skilfully wrapped around the body like a strapless dress). The men look fine in long ankle-length white robes. The countryside is some of the most beautiful we have seen, the earth intensely red, the green crops on the mango trees. Our garden has a small citrus Orchard and there is an enormous mango tree outside the kitchen door. The Bishop, our new boss, says we will miss all the fruits in South Africa: but we never had fruit like this place provides in our own garden.

December 15th

The children wear no shoes as they play outside, like our neighbours' children; but when they have their siesta, it does make a mess of the sheets (all stained red.)

December 31st

After Christmas, our fourth baby arrived, a few days earlier than expected. We call her Tessa Jill she's a little blonde girl, with a good pair of lungs judging from last night.

MASASI REFLECTIONS from Mkomaindo

Large windows without glass fit the weather, which is beautifully sunny and warm by the day, often rather too hot. It is never as hot

42

as Dar' because we are 1200 feet above sea level. There is a rainy season when it rains like clockwork at 2 pm for about an hour each afternoon. The earth dried as quickly as it had become wet. The night could be clammy and humid. Besides the nets at the windows, we slept in the mosquito nets in Tanzania. Malaria was common, especially among the Africans.

We took pills every week. I gave them to the children wrapped up in a spoon of jam. Some provisions are available from local Asian-run shops. The earth was fertile and there was a daily market selling good fresh fruit and vegetables. We bought our main provisions on six monthly visits to Lindi or Mtwara, a seaport where the wholesalers had a bigger variety, and cheaper prices too. We had a very nice manservant called a 'house boy' though older than me; he was also very efficient. He used to wash all the floors in the house every day. He also baked our bread. There was no baker's shop.

Soon after our arrival, we inherited a dog who had belonged to a departed member of staff. She was a huge Alsatian bitch, outstandingly friendly, docile. She was so gentle with the children and all our many visitors.

At Batlharos in our first 30 months, we did not see a single drop of rain.

We spent 2½ happy years in Tanzania. Our two oldest children became fluent in Swahili and were educated in Swahili. My husband enjoyed his work in the two hospitals. I think we were very privileged to be part of a different culture.

1994 - Oasis released, 'Definitely Maybe' and Blur, 'Parklife,' two records that captured the renewed hope of the nation emerging from a recession and possibly entering a new political era.

Life Begins Again, Near the End

Graham Albeck

Just after the war when times were hard
I helped out at a local builder's yard.
The hours were long and the pay was poor
So everybody there was wanting more.

I was born early in August in 1930
To my parents who were Fred and Girty.
And now much later on in life
I've a grown-up son and a loving wife.

I've got a nice house and drive a small car
And enjoy a few pints sat at the bar.
Fast forward now to the year 1995
And I count my blessings as I'm still alive.

I've got through life without much tension
Today I draw my first old age pension.
I've my ideas on some hobbies I intend doing
Join a walking club and maybe homemade brewing.

I feel the urge to travel and roam
I could buy myself a little motor home.
But, way back in time when writing was all the rage
You didn't live to a very old age.

Shelley and Keats only lived till twenty-nine
But between them they penned many a good line.

1994 – In Yokohama, Japan, the largest omelette in history was made,1383 square feet using 160,000 eggs.

The Day of the Fete

Mary Simpson

The village green was empty apart from the children's slide and the odd scrap of litter, lifted now and again by a gentle breath of wind. Alice parked alongside the village hall and looked around expecting there to be more people, someone from the committee, at least, to help with the trestle. It was early; the dew was still on the grass as she humped the trestle out of the car onto the green. Her children should be in the school gates by now. Her husband took them this morning to allow Alice to collect her bits and pieces together. She had been asked to help at the last minute as one of the stall holders had been taken ill.

At least she had first pitch. She positioned her stand on the north side, thinking it would be protected from the sun later on.

After 2 trips to her car collecting the stuff for her stall, she was amazed she had managed to accumulate so much; she noticed a tall well-built man out of the corner of her eye. He stood at the far end of the village hall. He was looking straight at her. There was something vaguely familiar about his stance and she wondered where she had seen him before.

She made a final journey for the two remaining boxes; back at her patch, she proceeded to unpack carefully the little china knick-knacks. Looking across the field for the stranger, she felt a vague disquiet at failing to see him. She busied herself arranging her stuff, and caught sight of him again; he was making his way purposefully across the field. It looked as if he was coming towards her and at a rapid pace. He was nearly upon her when Mrs. Brown, who was setting up her stall, came across.

'Morning Alice, aren't we the early birds.'

'Hello Edna, your pies look gorgeous.'

45

'I'd like that little blue jug, Alice. I believe it's Coal Port! How much for the little gem?'

Alice noticed the big man had slowed his approach. Now he was nearer she could see his features, she remembered where she had seen him. He was the new security guard from her husband's bank. What was he doing here, he should be at work?

Mrs. Brown pointed to another piece of blue china. 'Love this, how much?'

'Give me £5 for the two pieces.'

'Done.'

Alice kept her eye on the guard as she wrapped the two pieces carefully, first in the newspaper and then in a carrier bag. He had not moved an inch further.

A few more helpers were arriving, busying themselves setting up their stalls. Someone had opened the hall door and a tea urn went in, trays of sandwiches and cakes, a box with RAFFLE written on the side in red biro, probably full of useless stuff people did not want to win, thought Alice. Someone else started to arrange the tables and chairs on the concrete square fronting the hall and pretty tablecloths to cover. The fete was starting to come together and it was getting busy, with games being set up – a coconut shy, catch the apple, shove halfpenny.

'Here's your money Alice.'

'Do you want any of my pies before they all go?'

'I'll have a couple of apple. Did you say they were two pounds each?'

She glanced up and found herself looking into the steely eyes of the security guard. 'Hello,' she said as normal as possible, her heart was pounding; he had really made her jump. 'Is there anything I can get you? I've got some pretty things for sale today.'

He came quickly round to her side of the stall. 'You're coming with me.'

'Coming with you, what on earth do you mean, I'm on this stall. This is the village fete day. We are raising money for the upkeep of the hall. Why are you not at work?'

'His voice became menacing. 'If you want to see your husband and children again, walk to the end of the field and get in the black Mercedes!'

'Husband and children?' Her heart felt as if it would jump out of her body. 'What are you talking about?'

He grabbed her arm, making her wince, and propelled her towards the car. Dazed, she snatched up her bag off the end of the stall as she was hurried along.

Mrs Brown looked on in amazement, she had heard snatches of what was said 'husband and children' and she also noticed how pale Alice had become. She waited until they disappeared round the corner of the village hall and began to follow them. When she reached the hall she peered cautiously round the corner and saw Alice being pushed into the back seat of a black Mercedes but it was not the same man she had seen pushing Alice away from her stall. My God, she is being kidnapped. She felt in her pocket for a pencil. Dam, she had left it on her stall.

'FY57EMS' she said the registration number and kept repeating it.

She turned, thinking she would get back to her stall and get her mobile. She walked right into the arms of the security guard. Before she could get out of the way, she saw his grinning face as he brought something heavy down on her skull, and as she fell to the floor, her head reeling, she heard him running and then the car door slamming shut.

The car with its frightened passenger drove off at speed.

Alice had been pushed to the floor and held there by the guard's knee in her back. Although frightened, she was not given to panic and tried to assess the situation. John had gone to work as normal, taking both their children to the end of the road and they had only about a hundred yards into the school gates. She normally walked with them herself but she had agreed at the last minute to man the white elephant stall so John had taken them on his way to work.

Surely nothing could have happened in that hundred yards. No this thug was trying to frighten her and he'd succeeded, she was scared stiff.

She shuffled to get the weight on the other knee. The guard felt her movement and forced her further into the floor. Her bag was between her knees. She routed around for her mobile, please let it be there, got it, slipping it out and pushing it into the top of her blouse, making sure it was wedged in place by her bra.

She felt the car move right, out of Green Street, where the village hall was situated, and then a quick turn left Donnington Street, she thought. Another turn left Coronation Road, Milton Road, sharp turn left again into Meredith Road. They're taking me home!

'What you doing in your bag?' He snatched it from her.

'Not trying to use your mobile, I hope?' He pulled the bag up and pressed down harder in her back with his foot, he enjoyed the feeling of power, even with a defenceless woman. He searched round the bag and after satisfying himself it contained no 'phone he dropped it back on the floor.

The car was in her drive now and the big man was pushing her out, she landed unceremoniously on her knees in the gravel.

'Hurry up, don't hang about. Don't make a sound. Get into the house.'

Alice shuddered involuntarily, this man was a brute and she feared for herself and her children. The front door opened and a short, thin man stage whispered,

'What kept you?'

'A bit of trouble at the hall, Bill, a busybody was on the trail, had to double back and deal with that.'

'You didn't kill anyone did you?'

'No, she'll just have a sore head for a day or two.'

'Are you sure? We know what you're like.'

Alice was pushed inside her own front door. Noticing the car driver stayed in the car. She was seriously worried about her children and wondered if the big thug was talking about Mrs. Brown. They forced her down the hall, into her own living room. There on the settee were Millie and Molly her twin children.

'Mummy, Mummy,' they cried running into her arms.

'Thank God you're safe my darlings. Are you both alright?'

'Yes,' Millie said, she was the eldest by five minutes, 'he just keeps telling us to keep quiet'.

'What's happening, Mummy?' Molly asked. 'We haven't been to school Mummy.'

'Don't worry darlings,' hugging them both again. The big man pushed them back to the sofa.

'Get down and don't move. Keep your mouths shut.'

'Are the safes empty yet, Bill?' Mr. Big and Mr. Little thought Alice.

At the hospital Mrs. Brown regained consciousness. She had a massive cut on the side of her head which had been sutured and there was an ugly bruise starting and swelling. She was confused, calling out. 'They've got Alice. She was pushed into the back of a black Mercedes!'

The policewoman outside the ward heard her cries and came to the bedside and took her hand.

'Don't worry Mrs. Brown, we'll find her but you must rest, you've had a nasty shock.'

'No, I'm ok. I've got the number, the car, over and over, I said it, couldn't write it down. Hit, I was hit by a man.' The policewoman took out her pad.

'If you could remember the registration number, Mrs Brown, it would be most helpful. These men are dangerous; we need to catch them without delay.'

'The number is, the number is' she hesitated alarmed; 'oh I'm sorry, oh my head.'

The policewoman's voice was calm she realiscd Mrs. Brown was stressed. 'Don't worry Mrs. Brown, it will come to you, calm down, try to relax, close your eyes and visualise. You followed Alice to the end of the building, you peered round the corner. You saw Alice being pushed into the black car. You saw the number plate; you repeated it over and over again. Now what do you see Mrs. Brown?'

Meanwhile, at Meridith Road, Alice Ryder tried to remain calm. These men were brutes, she had been roughly handled, and she must do nothing to anger them. Her children were safe for the moment but what had they done with her husband? She did not want to leave the children but if she could get to the lavatory and use her mobile, there might be a chance of alerting someone before any further damage was done. She would have to try. 'I need to go to the lavatory'.

Big and little looked at one another. 'You go with her,Bill, and keep an eye on her; I'll stay here with the brats!'

'Don't leave us Mummy, we don't want you to leave us with these men,' the twins pleaded, clinging to her.

'I won't be a minute my darlings, just stay here on the sofa, hold hands, and don't say anything'.

She stood up and the little man shoved her and she stumbled out of the lounge into the hall. Bill looked inside the toilet to ensure there was no escape route and then pushed her inside and then closed the door, muttering,

'Hurry up!'

Once in the loo she quickly moved the mobile from her bra. SOS – BANK ROBBERS, she tapped.

'What's keeping you, hurry up?'

'I'm coming.' HV US AT MERIDITH RD. GET COPS.

'Hurry up.' Bill shouted, banging on the door.

'I'm coming,' she slipped the mobile into her pocket opened the toilet door with one hand, and pulled the lavatory chain with the other. Bill pushed her back unceremoniously down the hall and into the lounge. The twins hugged her as she sat down and she held them both tightly; hoping with all her heart that John was safe and not being brutalised.

At the hospital Mrs. Brown sat up shouting and immediately fell back on her pillow, holding her head. I'd like to get my hands on that brute, she thought. Resting for a minute then slowly raising herself so she could see the policewoman through the glass panel of her room. She waved her arms to attract the PC.

Collins' attention and then lay back exhausted with the effort of getting up and the effect of the painkillers she had received.

PC Collins came hastily into the room. 'Calm yourself, Mrs. Brown. You've remembered the registration number haven't you?'

'Yes, yes I have it. It's FY57EMS!'

'Well done, Mrs. Brown! Now try to get some rest. We'll soon find your friend, I'm sure of it.'

Mrs Brown lay back and closed her eyes, fretting about the fete, and struggling with her confusion. They were going to have such a lovely day. Had she given Alice her pies? Were the police looking after their stalls? It was so important they raise money for the hall. Had she told the police lady everything? A description of Alice's husband, no not Alice's husband, they needed to know what that great brute who hit her looked like....

Alice squeezed the twins and smiled down at them. Molly was nodding off, although trying hard not to but her eyelids were drooping and Alice could feel her getting heavier against her side as she relaxed and eventually fell asleep.

Molly awoke with a start. Goodness. Alice gasped audibly. My mobile, I couldn't have switched it off in my haste to get out of the lavatory.

The two thugs stood as one. 'What's that? Is that yours Bill?'

'No it's *hers*!' They moved in unison and before she had chance to move, they were on her.

'Stand up.' Bill was fleecing her.

'There's no need for that, it's in my pocket.' She reluctantly handed over her 'phone. They pushed her down on the settee with force.

'What's on it, Harry?'

'The bitch must have texted in the lavatory.'

Harry was fiddling with the mobile and brought up the last message. 'You cow!' He pulled Alice up and smacked her hard across the face.

She tried not to cry but both twins screamed. 'Leave our mummy, don't hurt our mummy.'

'Ring Jake, tell him not to come here! We must go to the other venue.'

Bill fumbled for his mobile, striking the keys dramatically.

'Jake, this bitch of a wife has contacted someone on her mobile.'

Alice heard a few choice words.

'Don't come to Meridith Road, get to the other venue, we'll meet you there.'

Alice froze and broke into a cold sweat as she heard.

'Take the kids, tie her up, and leave her there.'

'No take me and leave the children, *please*!'

Harry came across, smacked her hard across the face again. 'Shut up bitch!'

Alice was really frightened now, I made things worse. I should not have phoned. Her mind was racing. What if they leave my children at the other venue? Oh my God, it could be even worse. Her troubled thoughts were interrupted when the big guard, called Harry, pulled her up forced her arms cruelly behind her back, and started to tie up her wrist, very tight. They are animals she thought, fearing for her children. 'Leave my children, please, please, they are so young.'

Harry pushed her down onto the settee, not saying a word. The men were leaving, pushing the screaming twins.

'Gag them, Bill, and tie that bitch to something solid.' Bill went out and came back with a heavy dining chair and proceeded to tie the distressed Alice to the chair. Ignoring the protestations and pleadings for her children. She heard the front door open and Harry came back into the room.

'Get a move on Bill.'

'Ok, Ok.'

As they left the room, Harry bent down and turned on the gas that supplied the gas fire in the room. Alice was a prisoner, turning to Alice,

'Bye, bye, dear,' he said grinning maliciously.

Alice's text message had been reported to the local police station. Alice's brother had given full details of the bank where her husband worked and they had been in time to apprehend the villains red handed. Alice's husband, safe himself was worrying about his wife and children.

'Mr. Ryder, a police car was despatched to Meridith Road as soon as we received the message from your brother-in-law, it should be there, don't worry we'll get them.

As the police car approached 65 Meridith Road, they were just in time to see the black Mercedes leave.

'Don't put the siren on Dick, just follow the car and don't lose it!'

The Mercedes headed up Meridith Road, picking up the major road at the end of Durban Drive and then the driver put his foot down.

'He's heading for the motorway, the number is FY57EMS. We are following at a distance and we need another unmarked car, we can't lose them now… Over'

The Mercedes turned left unexpectedly at the next left turning with the silent police car closely behind. It travelled some distance before turning off into what looked like a derelict farm house. The police car slowed and the officers saw the men alight, pulling the distressed children after them.

'There's no woman Andy, they must have left her at Meridith Road. Get on the radio, someone needs to get to Meridith Road pdq, she may be hurt.

The policeman updated headquarters of the current situation whilst the driver parked the car across the entrance to the farmhouse. They alighted without a sound and crept cautiously up the drive.

'Alice smelled the gas almost immediately and struggled with the ropes at her wrists. 'Bloody hell, these are so tight,' she said aloud to herself and she cried out in pain as she struggled to ease the rope cutting into her wrists. Panic struck her as the nauseous gas filled the room and she tried to jump the chair towards the fire. She was exhausted, the sweat dripping from her forehead and she was beginning to feel the effect of the gas. 'Keep going Alice, you can reach it,' she shouted, 'you're nearly there.' Comforted by her own voice she struggled on, and one more jump brought her nearer to the gas fire. Little by little she managed to get halfway across the room before she vomited. 'If I could only get my foot to the fire. She had just managed to ease the knob around a little bit when she heard the police siren, the crunch of tyres on the gravel, slamming of doors, and 'Thank God' they were in the house. 'They've got my children!' she screamed, choking as she was sick again and now near to hysteria.

'Don't worry; we'll just get you to hospital.'

The policeman was untying her hands.

'No, no I'm fine, my children, my children.'

'They're fine, Mrs Ryder, we've got them safe and your husband is safe too. Alice heard as she lost consciousness.

She awoke in hospital 'Where am I?'

'Don't be upset, dear, everything's fine now.

Not your fault dear!' said the patient, getting back into her own bed next to Alice's. 'We'll never forget the 30th of June and our day at the Fete!'

1994 – Kurt Cobain, lead singer, guitarist and songwriter of Nirvana, committed suicide. A dark moment for rock.

The Lottery of Life

Ian Walker

"Hello."

"Hi, it's me. I'll be home in about 20 minutes."

"OK. See you then."

It was coming up to 7 pm on a cold Friday evening in October. Edward was driving home to Grimsby from London, where he worked during the week. He always called his wife, Linda, to give her a heads up when he was getting close to home, so she knew she could start getting dinner ready.

Edward was 58 years old. He worked as a structural engineer for a large construction company. He was currently working in London as the senior structural engineer for the construction of a new business complex near Canary Wharf. He'd worked in construction since leaving university in the mid-80s. He was good at his job but knew he had reached his career zenith. He knew he would never become a manager or a director after working for the same construction company for many years. He didn't regret this – his personality didn't suit the 'fluffiness' he felt was needed for those roles – he was much better suited to solving technical challenges rather than dealing with 'people problems'. He did, however, regret the limitations that a lack of career progression had on his salary. He was by no means poorly paid, but he knew that if he had the 'fluffy skills' he could now be on a six-figure salary.

Edward didn't gamble, but like many people, he played the National Lottery. He had been in it from the start when the chances of winning the minimum prize were such that you'd win something every few weeks or months. Over the years the lottery rules had changed and Edward found that he won nothing other than the odd 'Lucky Dip'. If ever there was a misnomer, then this was it. He never had a Lucky Dip win anything other than, at best, another Lucky Dip.

Rather than give up on the lottery Edward decided to play a different game - Euro millions. This, like the original National Lottery game, delivered small prizes every few weeks or months, so Edward felt like he was getting some payback. Over the years Edward's winnings had ranged from a couple of pounds to over a hundred pounds on one occasion, but he knew that the chances that he would win big were miniscule. This didn't stop him dreaming though, especially as the Euro millions jackpot could sometimes be over a hundred million pounds!

Edward had met Linda at university, where they started dating. He was studying civil engineering; she was studying history. After university, Edward immediately started work for his current employer, which had sponsored him through his degree. Linda stayed on to study teacher's training and eventually got a job teaching history at a comprehensive school. The nature of Edward's work meant that he had no defined place of work – he usually worked at the construction site – so when Edward and Linda moved in together and later married, they chose to live close to Linda's place of work. This eventually led to them living in their current detached house in Grimsby.

Edward's car pulled onto the drive. He got out of the car, collected his coat, suitcase, and laptop bag from the boot, locked the car, and entered the house. As he hung up his coat in the hallway Linda came to greet him.

"Hi," said Edward, giving Linda a peck on the cheek.

"How was the drive?" Linda asked.

"Pretty good. Friday's always hell but once I got past Leicester the traffic thinned out considerably. It's good to be home" Edward replied.

Edward changed out of his work clothes into jeans and a sweatshirt while Linda finished preparing dinner. They sat together to eat while sharing a cold bottle of Sauvignon Blanc. Their conversation was sporadic and limited to observations about the news, the weather, and whether any of their four children had been in touch (they hadn't). After nearly 40 years together the passion had, for all intents and purposes, left their relationship. They slept in separate bedrooms and Edward couldn't remember the last time they had been intimate ("Maybe when we were on holiday in Tenerife in April?" he thought to himself). Edward and Linda cleaned up after dinner and then sat together in the living room.

"Fancy a film?" Edward asked.

"OK," Linda replied.

"Any idea what film?"

"A horror?"

"OK. I'll have a look to see what I can find."

After about 10 minutes of scrolling through horror films available on Netflix and Prime Video they eventually settled on a film about a possessed nun. It finished just after 10 pm.

"Well, that was better than I expected," said Linda.

"Your expectations must have been pretty low," replied Edward.

"I'm off to bed now. Would you like a drink?"

"A cup of tea, please."

Linda brought Edward his tea and went to bed. Edward stayed up to watch another film before calling it a night. Then he too went to his bed.

Edward woke just after 9 am on Saturday. He went to the toilet and then made himself a coffee. Linda was already up and had left the house to visit a friend with whom she went jogging every Saturday and Sunday morning. Edward returned to bed with his coffee and opened his emails. Amongst the new emails he had received since last checking was the one that always gave him a glimmer of excitement – "News about your ticket" from The National Lottery. Could this be the jackpot he was hoping for?

Edward had given serious consideration as to what he would do should he win the jackpot. He was not sure whether or not he would stay with Linda. He wanted to experience love and passion in his life and it was not clear whether he and Linda would ever have this type of relationship again. It was great when they were younger, but now they acted like good friends rather than lovers. And, of course, Linda was in her late 50s, and although she was by no means unattractive, she didn't quite have the allure of the 20-or-30-something-year-old women that Edward envisaged having a few million pounds in the bank might make available to him!

Edward had previously explored whether a lottery win would need to be shared with Linda should he choose to divorce her. There was, apparently, a difference between 'matrimonial' property, like the house they shared, and 'non-matrimonial' property that belonged solely to one party. As Edward played the lottery as an individual using funds from his sole bank account it seemed that any win would be his and his alone. At least that was his interpretation of what he had read.

Edward played both Tuesday and Friday draws and used the same numbers for each. Euro millions required five numbers between 1 and 50 plus two Lucky Star numbers between 1 and 12. He based his numbers on family birthdays – his birthday (2nd), Linda's birthday (11th), their four children's birthdays (13th, 17th, 18th, 28th) and his brother's birthday (31st). He never changed them as he couldn't handle the scenario where his numbers came up afterward. "Better to always lose than to suffer this experience," he thought.

Edward logged into his online National Lottery account and checked his winnings. He had won a grand total of £2.70! Not quite enough for his retirement! Oh well.

Saturday and Sunday continued with no excitement. The lottery win had been the highlight of his weekend. It was now 6 am on Monday and Edward was up, showered, dressed, fed, and watered. He left the house quietly, not wishing to disturb Linda, and got into his car ready for the 200-mile drive down to London.

Edward arrived at the construction site shortly before 11 am. He spent most of the next 7 hours in a variety of technical discussions and meetings before leaving to check into his hotel. His employer covered his travel and hotel costs, which meant he could afford to stay at the Canary Wharf Hilton hotel. He checked in, ate a three-course meal, and then settled into his hotel room for the evening. After checking his work and personal emails, he settled down to watch a film while drinking a glass of wine. In the earlier days of their marriage, Edward would have called Linda to discuss their day and wish each other goodnight, but this tradition had long since ceased.

Tuesday, Wednesday, Thursday, and Friday would be a repeat of Monday, except that Edward would be at the construction site at around 8 am. Tuesday to Thursday, at 6 pm, Edward would finish for the day and return to the hotel. On Friday Edward would finish work around 1 pm and embark on his 200-mile trip back to Grimsby. That, in a nutshell, was Edward's typical working week.

This week, however, was to be different. When Edward awoke on Wednesday morning and checked his personal emails, he found he had received a new "News about your ticket" email. He was half-awake when he checked what he had won using his online account but soon awoke when he read the amount - £75,922.10! He double-checked his online ticket against the numbers in Tuesday evening's draw just to make sure that there hadn't been a mistake. The numbers drawn were 13, 17, 18, 28, and 30 with 2 and 11 being the Lucky Stars. He had missed the jackpot by one number – his brother's birthday was 31st but 30 had been drawn. Still, 75 thousand pounds was not to be sniffed at.

During the week Edward thought more about his winnings and what he should do with them. It wasn't the millions he had dreamed of and certainly wasn't enough to divorce Linda and entice a 20-or-30-something-year-old woman to his side. He recalled the holiday in Tenerife, the last time he and Linda had been intimate. Maybe what was needed was for him and Linda to spend some quality time together, without the pressures of work or the mundaneness of daily life. Maybe there was still a chance to rekindle the fire and passion that they used to have.

Edward made a decision. Next week was half-term so Linda would not be at school. He quickly arranged to take next week off work and booked a week's holiday in Tenerife for himself and Linda. They would fly out on Sunday. He would surprise Linda with the news about the lottery win and the holiday on Friday evening when he got home from work.

During the drive home on Friday, Edward stopped off at Leicester Forest East services on the M1, where he knew there was a Waitrose. He bought flowers and champagne. He then continued his journey. When he reached Caenby Corner he called Linda. Linda answered the phone.

"Hello."

"Hi, it's me. I'll be home in about 20 minutes."

"OK. See you then."

Edward was smirking to himself. What would Linda's reaction be when he walked in with the flowers and champagne and told her of his lottery win? In twenty minutes, he would find out.

Edward's car pulled onto the drive. He got out of the car and collected his coat, suitcase, and laptop bag from the boot. He then picked up the flowers and champagne from the back seat and locked the car. He entered the house and hung up his coat in the hallway. Linda did not come to greet him.

He left the suitcase and laptop bag in the hallway and entered the kitchen with the flowers and champagne in hand. Linda was by the sink and looked rather surprised by Edward's accoutrements.

"What are they for?" she asked.

"Do we need an excuse for champagne and flowers?" Edward replied.

He put the flowers and champagne down on the kitchen table and walked over to Linda, intending to kiss her. He was surprised to see her back away. He decided to explain what was going on.

"I bought the flowers and champagne because I love you and I want us to rekindle our relationship. I remember how we were in Tenerife in April and I want us to go back there next week and pick up where we left off. I know that we've been growing apart but I think we still have a chance, a very good chance, if we both want it and if we both invest more time into our relationship."

Linda was taken aback. She was surprised and shocked by Edward's statement. Not because it wasn't true, but because she had come to the conclusion that their relationship was over. For her, the intimacy in Tenerife had been a last attempt to test their love for each other and it had failed. She had moved on.

"I need to tell you something," she said. "For some time now, I've realised that our relationship was coming to an end. I have found love with someone else. It has just been a matter of timing as to when to tell you and now is the right time. I've come into some money and can now afford to leave you. You can keep everything – the house, the car – I'm going to start afresh."

"What money?" asked Edward.

"Well, I see no harm in telling you," Linda replied. "You see I've been playing Euro millions for some months now. I used our birthdays, the kid's birthday, and my sister's birthday as the numbers, and this week they came up."

Edward's mind was whirring. The numbers were the same as his except for her sister's birthday. What date is her sister's birthday? Then he remembered – the 30th of September – 30, the number he didn't have.

"You won the jackpot?" he asked, already knowing the answer.

"Yes," she replied. "124 million pounds."

Edward sat down on one of the kitchen chairs. "Bloody hell!" he said. "I was going to tell you that I'd won 75 thousand pounds. That's small change to you now."

Linda carried on speaking. "I waited for you to get home so that I could tell you face-to-face that it's over. I'm leaving now. I'm sorry that things have turned out this way but you know as well as I do that we have been living as friends and not husband and wife for some time now. I still love you, but I no longer desire you. Take care."

With that, Linda opened the front door and left the house. Edward could hear her get into a car and then he heard the car drive away.

"Shit!" he thought. What the hell was he to do now? Maybe he could go after some of Linda's winnings? But then he remembered his research. This was a 'non-matrimonial' asset and he didn't have any claim to it. What was he to do? He threw the flowers in the bin and opened the champagne. It was going to be a long night of drinking.

Edward was awakened by a loud knocking at the front door. He glared at the clock until he could read it. It was 5:15 am. He staggered to his feet, put on his dressing gown, and made his way to the front door. When he opened the door, he found himself face-to-face with a policeman and a policewoman.

"Is this the home of Linda Wilkins?" the policeman asked.

"Er, yes," Edward answered.

"May I ask who you are?" the policeman responded.

"I'm Edward Wilkins, Linda's husband."

"May we come in?"

"Er, OK," Edward replied. "Do you want a coffee? I'm going to make myself one."

"No thank you, sir," was the reply. "Perhaps you should sit down?"

Edward led the policeman and policewoman into the living room and sat down. "What is this all about?" he asked.

The policeman coughed. "I'm afraid we have some very bad news. Your wife was involved in a car accident this evening and I'm afraid the prognosis is not good. She was the passenger in a car being driven by a man. We believe that he had been drinking and unfortunately, he lost control of the car. He was killed instantly. Your wife is critically ill in hospital. We can take you there now. Is there anyone else we should inform? Is there anyone you would like to call?"

Edward was desperately trying to sober up and take in what was being said to him. "Who was the man?" he asked.

The policeman checked his notebook. "David Roberts. Do you know him?"

Edward scanned his memory but the name was not familiar to him. "No" he replied.

"He was a teacher at the same school as your wife," continued the policeman.

"Was this Linda's new love?" Edward thought. "We should go to the hospital," he said. He went upstairs, dressed, and re-joined the police in the living room. "Let's go," he said.

It took about 20 minutes to reach Scunthorpe General Hospital from Edward's home. The police took Edward into the A&E Department where they were escorted to a side-room. After a few minutes, a doctor entered the room.

"Mr Wilkins?" he asked.

"Yes," Edward replied. "How is Linda?"

"It's my sad duty to tell you that Linda passed away a few minutes ago. I'm afraid that her injuries were just too severe for her to survive. I'm sorry."

Edward sat quietly for a moment.

"Is there anyone we should call for you?" the policeman asked.

"No," Edward replied. "Please can you take me home?"

Thirty minutes later Edward was back at his home. The police had left and he was alone. He has sobered up considerably in the past couple of hours. It was now 7 am and Edward had a cup of coffee in his hand. He now had to call his children to let them know that their mother had died. He decided to construct a story about Linda being out with a work colleague for purely innocent purposes. There was no point in adding further pain to the grief that his children were going to feel.

As for himself, he was certainly distressed by what had happened, but he had figured out that this cloud had a silver, if not golden, lining. He was the sole beneficiary of Linda's will. He may never have got his hands on any of the 124 million pounds had Linda lived, but now that she was dead, it would all be his!

1994 - The film The Shawshank Redemption, adapted from a Stephen King novel, won multiple awards.

Does Crime Pay?

Jean Willett

The gates slammed shut behind Pete Smith as he walked out of prison.

"Try not to come back," shouted one of the warders at Pete as he almost skipped to a nearby bus stop. "No chance," thought the released prisoner. Pete was nearly forty-nine and had spent half of his life behind bars but he had plans, plans he had made before he had even been caught for this crime.

He jumped off the bus close to the hostel he was to stay in for the next six months. And then, providing he had behaved himself he would be free to go wherever he wanted to. The hostel was clean, his room was comfortable and he soon settled into life on the outside. He managed to secure a part-time job washing up in a small café and the rest of his time was his own.

Pete enjoyed reading but spent a lot of his time thinking about his past. He'd been born the youngest of seven children four boys and three girls. As the youngest, he'd been his mother's favourite and she often saved him from the wrath of his bullying father. Whenever he did something wrong his mother would play down his role in the misdemeanour and direct it to one of his older brothers so consequently, his brothers took against him.

 Pete was sincere in his plans to go straight; he'd had enough of prison life and food. Once he'd achieved the next step in his plans he'd live his life as he wanted, not as he was told. He'd spent the last six months planning his future and regretting his past but everything depended on one thing.

The last crime he had committed had yielded a large amount of money, enough for him to start up a car hire firm, one that provided cars for special events such as weddings and proms. It was a business he'd always dreamed of owning and running.

Long before they were caught, he and his partner in crime had buried their ill-gotten gains in a safe place, an elderly neighbour's back garden. Ready to be retrieved when they were released. As he was totally deaf the old man was hardly likely to hear them in the middle of the night.

Unfortunately, his partner and friend had suffered a heart attack in prison so the money was now his alone.

The street name was easy to remember but to make sure he got the right house he'd had the number 30 tattooed on his wrist. He was often asked what the number meant and his stock reply was that it was his mother's birthday.

After leaving the hostel he decided to go and suss out the place where his future fortune was hidden. He took a bus to the small market town he'd grown up in and with a cocky swagger in his walk he strolled up to Henry Street. As he turned the corner his face paled, one side of the street had been demolished in its place stood a brand-new leisure centre.

Six months later, Pete was once more entering the prison gates, the guard who had waved him out was now booking him. He smiled ruefully as he said, "Thought we weren't going to see you anymore, Pete, welcome back."

1994 - This is the year Amazon and Yahoo appeared on the internet.

Covid 19

Christine McCrae

Covid came along
And raced through the world,
Catching anyone too close,
A nightmare of epic proportions,
Frightening, alarming and scary.
No one could stop it at first,
We tried our best
But many died
Thousands.
Some had stifling, choking deaths
A monstrous tragedy.
Then Pfizer and Astra Zeneca
Developed the solution
A vaccine.
Two jabs, well- spaced, twelve weeks apart.
And so we started to feel
That with restrictions,
With lockdown and this healing jab
We were starting to beat this monster.
Time passed, people furloughing
And many shops closed
For months.
We could catch it again in 30 days
So better be careful.
Now here we are
Moved to a safer place
A place with variant threats

But the best place yet.
A place of normality
A time to be happy again
And we were grateful.

1994 – 'Friends,' The US Sitcom was introduced to our TV screens, capturing the optimism and aspirations of urban twenty-somethings.

The Reunion

Alan Gilbert

I needed to be there by midnight. That gave me almost 40 minutes. Ahead, the street was deserted though the occasional car would roar or rumble on the road behind me. To my right was a seemingly endless terrace of homes, yet to be condemned. More nervous than I had ever been in my life, my steps became slower and softer as I approached the final one. My wife, who was at home some 90 miles away, believed I was visiting an old friend. It wasn't a complete lie.

I stopped just short of the corner of the block and peered round it. Less than 50 metres long, the end of the street was blocked by an ancient wrought iron gate that was never opened. Behind it hid a school for the sons of the wealthy. Facing the few houses on this street though, was a much grander pair of gates. The entrance to Westside Park, a vast council-owned area of football pitches, tennis courts, miniature golf, flowers, bushes and places for children to play.

Next to the gates was a chest-high brick wall which, years before, I had been able to scale with ease. Once over the wall I would be committed to my mission there was a high probability that no one would be there. The reunion had been planned exactly 30 years earlier. I had remembered but had he long since forgotten? For the sake of Debbie and Becky though, I had to make the meeting.

I cautiously approached the wall, scanning the houses facing it for signs of life. Could someone be looking out of their window? If they saw me would they call the police? I tried to scale the wall using my old technique and fell in a painful heap. Doubts surged through my mind. What was I doing? Why hadn't I come better prepared?

My right knee was aching as I rose from the ground and approached the gates. In the limited light, the brickwork looked perfect with no footholds. 'You idiot,' I grunted to myself, why didn't you check earlier?' The gates seemed to rise into the sky but by rotating my feet a little, my shoes just fitted between the bars and so I slowly climbed. Reaching the top of the gates was unthinkable. I transferred one foot to the wall, then the other. I was standing on masonry that wasn't exactly rigid. It slid a little before plunging downwards and surfing its way through foliage whilst depositing me on a vicious, leafed monster. My ankle was twisted and I could feel blood on my back.

For a while, I dared not move. I had yelled as I landed and surely woken someone. But, there was a desperate need to extricate myself from this wooden dagger. With some difficulty, I slowly stood and peered over the top of the wall. The houses remained in darkness. I took one step and was standing on tarmac. With my back to the centre of the gates, I began to limp blindly forward. The path was wide enough for a car but only council motor vehicles were allowed here. In the total darkness, I moved in agony along what I felt was a straight line but, after a few steps was tripped by a small bush. I stood up and switched on my little torch hoping that no one would be able to see me now.

On both sides of the path were small bushes and trees. Beyond them were tall railings. To my right was the school and to my left a cemetery. I moved to the centre of the path and continued my slow, painful journey. Eventually, the railing to my left disappeared and the ground rose slightly, I was there but it was ten minutes after 12. This grassed area known as The Hump was the only hill in the park. Hobbling into the blackness, the torchlight revealed a shelter, still standing after all of these years. I toppled onto a hard wooden bench.

Had he been and gone or was I just being stupid? Then I heard someone chuckling.

'You've let yourself go, Ralph.'

'Hello, Reggie.'

'Good to see you my old mate. I didn't think you'd come.'

'I wasn't sure about you either.'

'We made a solemn promise to meet at midnight exactly 30 years after leaving school.'

'You could have suggested somewhere a little easier to get to, Reggie.'

'I was planning ahead, Ralph, you know what the situation is with me.'

'Yes, Reggie.'

'It was fun watching you. I bet you've ruined your clothes. I came in through the boneyard. It has a much lower fence and you just walk through a gap in the wall to get into the park.'

'You checked the place out in advance?'

'Of course Ralph, didn't you?'

'I didn't finish work until six and then I had a long drive to get here.'

'I am self-employed of course.'

'Yes, and I suppose you had a good meal somewhere.'

'Haven't you eaten, Ralph?'

'Not since lunchtime.'

'Come on then, let's get to the caff.'

'I don't think it's open, Reggie,' I said light-heartedly. At that, a powerful torch was switched on.

'Don't be daft mate. Nothing's ever closed to me.' We descended the hill using Reggie's beam of light. There it was, the old cafe. Well, not so old now, the ancient wooden shed had been replaced by a brick structure. Shutters covered the windows but Reggie's only interest was the door, which had two locks. The large torch was switched off and a smaller one began shining out of his top pocket. An L-shaped piece of rod was inserted into one lock and after a few rotations, taken out.

'That's careless of them, they've only used one lock. Right Ralph, don't move until I give the all-clear.' He opened the door and walked in.

'It's OK Ralph,' he shouted, 'the idle buggers haven't even switched the alarm on. Come in.'

Reggie began switching lights on and off until he was happy with the level of illumination. 'What do you fancy Ralph?'

'I suppose it's a burger and sausage place?'

'Yep, I think it is but, I bet they've got some nice cakes and chocolate bars.' A handful of wrapped cakes and chocolate fell onto the table. Reggie sat down facing me.

'I suppose you've heard about me?' he asked.

'Not until about five years ago.'

'What was it, a newspaper or the TV?'

'Neither, it was Ed Grower.'

'He didn't become a Copper did he?'

'No, he started out as an electrician but ended up as the County Police Estate Manager. He saw your picture in one of the stations.'

'Was it a good likeness?'

'I haven't seen it but apparently, it was one of those computer-generated things.'

'That's good, no real photographs.'

'So your specialty is breaking into rich peoples' homes is it?'

'I mainly go for stately homes and manor houses. I have become quite an authority on rare paintings and antiques. Rich private collectors can also be a good source of both, of course. I'm a modern Robin Hood.'

'Do you distribute your earnings amongst the poor then?'

'No, I am the poor.'

'Are you still short of money after this many years?'

'No, I own property in three different countries. I also do well with shares.'

'You have injured people.'

'Look, you don't expect lackeys to fight to save their master's wealth. That's being really stupid and so they get what they deserve.' At this point, Reggie probably didn't like the way the conversation was heading and decided to change the subject.'

'Do you remember old Coxlin?'

'Our form tutor?'

'Yes, he was always going on at me. He said I was a waster and would never amount to anything. Well look at me, I am at the top of the heap and look what happened to him. I showed him, didn't I?'

'What do you mean?' I asked.

'I did his place over.'

'That was you then, wearing a mask?'

'Yep, of course, it was.'

'Did you have to frighten his daughter like that?'

'She was his daughter, so she deserved it.'

'Becky was only twelve and you forced her to go round the house with you as you trashed everywhere. You particularly enjoyed wrecking her room. She is still too frightened to stay in a house on her own.'

Reggie was suddenly silent. He stared at me for several seconds before speaking.

'How do you know all this, Ralph?'

'I married Becky's sister. When Debbie first took me home, her dad threw me out. But, she stood by me, and eventually Mr Coxlin accepted that I wasn't like you.'

'What's going on here, Ralph?'

'It's the end of the road, Reggie.'

Suddenly two doors burst open and policemen surrounded the table. Reggie genuinely looked shocked as he was handcuffed. 'How could you do this to a mate Ralph?' he pleaded.

'We were never mates, Reggie. You always sat by me in the form. You insisted on walking home with me because I had to pass your house and you hid with me on The Hump when I was bunking off football. We were known as the Two R's and nobody spoke to me. They thought I was just like you.'

'OK but there is something,' he said.

'What's that?'

'Why were the cops hiding in here? How did they know we'd be in here?'

'I knew that out in the open, the police would never catch you, but here they couldn't fail.'

'But how...?'

'I told you I was hungry, and you could never resist showing off.'

1994 - The case against O.J. Simpson, the American footballer, began to form. Accusing him of the murders of his ex-wife and her friend.

Serendipity

Ian Walker

John re-read the message on his phone.

"The first murder was as easy as pie but had no point. The second murder will be perfect."

He'd read the text at least a dozen times but he couldn't make sense of it. John liked puzzles, especially word and number puzzles, but he couldn't make head-nor-tail of this one.

John was a detective working for Humberside Police. He was based in Grimsby, North East Lincolnshire. A few days ago, the local newspaper named him the lead detective working on a murder case. He'd been pictured at the crime scene and had responded with the standard 'nothing to report at this time'. The following day he received the text. It had been sent from a pre-paid phone. There was no way to trace the phone's owner. With the help of the mobile network operator, they had been able to trace where the text was sent from, but this proved to be of little use. It was sent from Blundell Park, Grimsby Town's football ground when a match was being played. The official attendance figure for the match was over 5,000.

Early on the morning of 4th August 2017, the body of a man had been recovered from Alexandra Dock. It had initially appeared to be a case of accidental drowning. The post-mortem had identified high levels of alcohol in the blood and it was almost dismissed as an accident until a puncture wound was detected at the base of the skull just beneath the hairline. Further blood tests detected traces of Curare, which when injected into the bloodstream could cause paralysis or even death. The hypothesis now was that the man had been poisoned with Curare before being lowered into Alexandra Dock, where he drowned. He would not have been able to swim due to paralysis.

This was a highly unusual crime for Grimsby. Most violent crimes were spontaneous, involved young men, and were drug or alcohol related. This crime appeared to be premeditated and sophisticated in its execution.

It was not clear if the text was genuine or a hoax. The problem was, though, if it was genuine, it suggested that there would be a second murder. What's more, the wording suggested something more. What was a "perfect" murder, and why was the first murder "as easy as pie"? Perhaps John was overthinking things and it was some idiot who thought he was clever by texting him. What puzzled him, however, was how the texter obtained his mobile phone number.

It was now the evening of 6th August. Inquiries into the murder were continuing but there was very little to go on. The body had no means of identification. There was no wallet or phone and his fingerprints and DNA were unknown to the police. Information had been shared with Interpol but nothing had come back as yet.

John's mobile phone rang. It was from Sharon, one of the other detectives assigned to the case. "Hi," he answered.

"There's been another one," Sharon said.

"Another what?"

"Another body has been found. It's too early to tell if it's murder but it fits the same MO."

"Where do I need to be?"

"A car is on its way to pick you up. The body was found washed up at Cleethorpes Beach. I'll meet you there."

"OK."

After a couple of minutes, a marked car arrived and took John to the location where the body had been found. SOCO had cordoned off part of the beach close to The Boating Lake and they were combing the area for evidence. A forensic pathologist was examining the body. On seeing John, he left the body and walked towards him. Sharon was by his side.

"What do we have?" John asked.

"It looks the same," replied the pathologist. "I checked the base of the skull and can see a puncture wound. We'll need the post-mortem to confirm, but I guess that it's the same as the other body."

"OK. Keep me informed," John turned to Sharon. "Anything to report on the crime scene?"

"Not yet. There are no obvious signs of a person's presence around the body, but of course, the sea is great at washing away any evidence that there might have been."

At that moment John's phone pinged. He had received a new text. He took out his phone and read it.

"The third murder will almost be worth its weight in gold." he read out loud.

He paused for a moment and then spoke again. "You know what this means. The first text wasn't a hoax and there's going to be another murder!"

He spoke to Sharon: "Meet me at the incident room tomorrow at 8 am with whatever SOCO has come up with."

He then spoke to the pathologist: "When can I expect the results of the post-mortem?"

"Once the body is released to me it'll take a few hours. I'll rush through the blood tests to confirm Curare was used. I should have the results sometime tomorrow afternoon."

John left the crime scene and returned to his home in the patrol car. Tomorrow was going to be a busy day. Not only did he have two murders on his plate, he was now expecting a third. And he still had no idea what the wording of the texts meant.

The following morning, at 8 am, John entered the incident room at Grimsby Police Station. In attendance were Sharon and Paul, a third detective who had been assigned to the original murder case. Julie and David, two younger officers who were helping on the case, were also present.

"Good morning," John said.

"Good morning, sir."

"OK. Let's start with the new body. What do we know about him?"

"He's a Caucasian male in his late forties or early fifties, in decent physical shape, about 6 feet tall. There was nothing on the body to identify him and his fingerprints and DNA are unknown. We've sent them off to Interpol and are waiting to hear back. It's just like the first body." Paul replied.

"Anything from SOCO?"

"Nothing of any use. The location means that any evidence of a third party would have been washed away. It could also be that the body washed up and that the murder was committed elsewhere." Sharon replied.

"Any new news on the first murder?"

"No. Nothing." Said Sharon. "We're still waiting for a response from Interpol on his DNA and fingerprints. House-to-house is continuing around the area of Alexandra Dock. And we've checked for any CCTV footage and found nothing relevant."

John paused for thought.

"OK. The bodies and the crime scenes aren't revealing much so far. But we do have one more thing to go on. It appears that the murderer may be contacting me by text."

He took a piece of paper out of his pocket and pinned it to the evidence board.

"This is a printout of the texts I have received."

"The first murder was as easy as pie but had no point"

"The second murder will be perfect."

"The third murder will almost be worth its weight in gold."

"Surely they are just hoax texts?" said Paul. "Why would the murderer be sending you texts?"

"That was my initial thought," replied John, "But there's no way that a hoaxer would know about the second murder. How could they send me a text about a third murder just after the second body was found?"

"Maybe it was someone who saw the police presence, saw you arrive at the crime scene, and put two-and-two together? It could still be a hoaxer," responded Paul.

John thought about this possible explanation. "You're right," he said. "The texts could still be from a hoaxer, but whoever they are from, I think you're onto something. I received the text about the third murder when I was attending the crime scene of the second. I bet whoever sent the text was watching the crime scene and saw my arrival. We need to trace where the second text originated from."

"On it, Sir," said David.

"OK," John continued, "I still think that the texts are from the murderer. I think he is giving us clues about the murders. We need to try and decipher them. We already know about the first two murders, so how can we connect the first two clues with these murders?"

"Assuming that the clues align with the murders of course," queried Sharon.

"What do you mean?"

"What if we're missing a murder? Or what if there's more than one murderer?"

"The timing of the texts is too closely aligned with the two murders we have. Let's not complicate things. Let's work on the assumption that the texts are clues from the murderer and relate to the murders we know about. OK?"

"OK."

"What do we know about the first murder?" John continued.

Paul stood up. "He's a Caucasian male in his late forties or early fifties, overweight, about 5'9" tall. There was nothing on the body to identify him and his fingerprints and DNA are unknown. His body was discovered on 4th August but the post mortem indicates that he was murdered on the 3rd. His body was found in Alexandra Dock. He had drowned after being injected with Curare."

"How is any of that related to 'as easy as pie but had no point'?" asked Sharon.

"Maybe he bakes pies for a living? Maybe his life was pointless?" chimed in Julie, with a hint of sarcasm in her voice.

John gave Julie a stern look before continuing. "What about the second murder? What do we know about that one?"

Paul spoke again. "He's a Caucasian male in his late forties or early fifties, in decent physical shape, about 6 feet tall. There was nothing on the body to identify him and his fingerprints and DNA are unknown. He was murdered on 6th August. His body was found at Cleethorpes Beach close to The Boating Lake. We are presuming that he had drowned after being injected with Curare. We should get confirmation of this this afternoon."

"So why was this murder perfect?" asked Sharon. "Or why is this murder any more perfect than the first murder? What makes them different from each other?"

"If we ignore the victim for a moment, the only difference seems to be the date and location. Even the cause of death appears to be the same," John responded.

There was silence for a few moments, then David coughed and spoke. "I've just noticed something, sir. I remember from school that 6 is a perfect number. The murder took place on the 6th so maybe this is what the clue was alluding to?"

"What's a perfect number?" asked Sharon.

"It's a number equal to the sum of its divisors, excluding itself," replied David.

"In English?" asked Sharon again.

"OK. Six is equal to 1 times 6 and 2 times 3. If you ignore the 6, the factors are 1, 2, and 3. Add 1, 2, and 3 together and you get 6. So, six is a perfect number."

John thought about this. It fitted the clue but seemed a bit tenuous. What about the first clue?

"OK. Let's assume that the clue relates to the date. How does 'as easy as pie but had no point' lead us to the 3rd?"

There was silence for a few seconds, and then David spoke again. "It's pi, sir. The number pi I mean. Pi is 3.1416-ish, so if you drop anything after the decimal point you get 3. The 3rd."

Everyone was silent for a few seconds and then John spoke.

"OK. The logic is a little tenuous but it seems to work. At least for the first two murders. How can we use this to help us identify when the third murder will be? What does 'almost worth its weight in gold' mean? How can we derive a date from this clue?"

"Maybe it's a golden wedding anniversary? 50 years?" suggested Sharon.

"50 is too big a number to follow the pattern. If it's a date it must be 31 or less," answered Paul.

"I'm just Googling 'gold' sir. Give me a minute," said Julie.

"From Wikipedia," she continued, "Gold is a chemical element.....atomic number 79.....group 11 element..... its specific gravity is 19.3......".

"What does specific gravity mean?" interrupted Sharon.

"It's a measure of density," replied David. "A specific gravity of 19.3 means that gold is 19.3 times heavier than water, which has a specific gravity of 1."

"It's a measure of weight then," said Sharon, "didn't the text mention weight?"

"' The third murder will almost be worth its weight in gold'," said John. "That was the text. So, if we assume that the next murder will be on the 19th, we have 12 days to try to prevent it."

The post-mortem of the second body confirmed that the victim had been injected with Curare, the same as the first victim. Over the next 12 days' inquiries continued, but with little to go on no progress was made in identifying the victims, the motive, or the killer. There had been no reports of missing persons that matched the description of the bodies.

The second text had been sent from the Promenade, close to the pier, a vantage point from which it would have been possible to keep an eye on the second crime scene, but far enough away to not be suspicious. CCTV of the area had been examined but nothing useful was found. There were far too many people using their phones to identify any individual suspect. Car registrations had also been traced but follow-up interviews had found no suspicious activity related to any of the vehicles involved.

The phone used by the killer was only ever turned on to make these specific texts meaning it could not be traced by the network operator.

Investigations into the Curare poison had also proved ineffective. It was, apparently, a poison that anyone with sufficient knowledge could make, as long as they had access to the relevant plant extracts. Some of these plant extracts were available to purchase online, many being associated with some curative properties when used in low doses, for which they were purportedly sold.

Consideration had been given as to whether a public announcement should be made, warning the public that a similar crime might be committed on 19th August, but this had been rejected. With nothing to go on regarding the location, suspect, or potential victim there was nothing of any real substance to state in a warning. It could even make matters worse by suggesting that the police were dumbfounded in their efforts to find the killer. It would also reveal to the killer that their texts had been deciphered. If this caused the texts to stop, it might prevent the killer from revealing something significant that he would otherwise have done in a later text.

The 19th of August had now arrived. Police had been brought in from the surrounding area to patrol around the dock and the coastline, but given how extensive these areas are they could not guarantee to spot, let alone prevent, a third murder.

It was 10:15 pm when John received a call from Sharon.

"He's struck again, Sir. Cars on its way."

John was collected and taken to Grimsby Leisure Centre. He was met by Sharon.

"The body's in the changing rooms. It looks like he was getting ready to swim when the killer struck," she said.

"OK. He's struck in a less secluded place. Hopefully, we can find some evidence this time!" replied John. "Do they have CCTV?"

"Yes," replied Sharon, "though not in the changing rooms for obvious reasons."

"Does it cover the entrance and exit?"

"Yes. We've already requested the recordings for today. We shut down the leisure centre when the body was found so nobody has left since."

"How many people?"

"About forty. What do you want to do with them?"

"For now, we just need a statement from each of them. I bet nobody saw anything. Make sure we get everyone's identity and double-check it. We also need to check everyone's phone to see if it matches the one used by the killer. There's always a chance that the killer is amongst them."

Just then John's phone pinged again. Another text.

"Here we go!" he said. He opened the text and read it out loud.

"The odds on the fourth murder are thirty in a thousand."

"Can we check if anyone was seen texting just now? Maybe he just made a big mistake!" said John.

"We took everyone's phone off them as a precaution," replied Sharon. "Everyone is being held in the main sports hall. I'll check to see if anyone saw anyone use a phone that hadn't been turned in."

Sharon set off to the sports hall. John headed to the changing room, where he met Paul and the forensic pathologist.

"We have to stop meeting like this," said the pathologist. "It looks the same as before. The same puncture wound. I'll confirm after the post-mortem tomorrow."

"OK. Thanks," replied John. "Have SOCO come up with anything this time?" he asked Paul.

"We think that the killer waited in one of the cubicles until his victim was alone. He could have waited some time. People don't tend to interfere with anyone who appears to be changing in a cubicle. We're checking for fingerprints but with wet tiles and a lot of comings and goings this is likely to prove fruitless."

Sharon entered the room. "Nobody saw anyone texting from the sports hall and there's no evidence that anyone is concealing a second phone. I think we have to presume that the text came from somewhere else and not one of the forty people we have detained."

"OK. Process them and give them back their phones. We'll pick this up tomorrow at the incident room and review what we have. We need to decipher the new text, though to be honest, even if we decipher it, it probably won't help us."

At 8 am the following morning the team were convened in the incident room.

"Good morning."

"Good morning, sir."

"OK. We have a new victim and a new text. We will have the results of the post-mortem later today but I think it's fair to assume that it's the same MO as before. What do we know about the victim?"

Paul stood up. "His name is Robert Jones. He's 68 years old. He's retired. He has no criminal record. He lives alone. We have people looking around his house but so far nothing of interest has come up. He's just an old man, sir. He doesn't seem to do anything that would warrant his murder. Maybe he's just unlucky and happened to be alone in the changing rooms at the wrong time."

"That would seem to fit the pattern of the first two murders. There's no obvious connection between the victims. They're just random men," said Sharon.

"I agree up to a point," responded John, "but this is the first victim we have been able to identify, so how can we be sure that there's no connection between them? We need to dig more into Robert

Jones's life. Maybe we can find a motive for his murder somewhere in his past. Julie, can you get onto this please?"

"Yes, sir," she replied.

"We also have a new text to decipher. 'The odds on the fourth murder are thirty in a thousand.' Anyone got any ideas?"

David spoke. "Based on the previous clues we expect the answer to be a date. We therefore know that the answer is a number from one to thirty-one."

"Agreed," replied John, "but how does a date have odds? Don't all dates have the same odds?"

"They can't have," chimed in Sharon. "February is weird for a start. Twenty-eight days for three years and then twenty-nine days for a year."

"It's even weirder than that," said David. "If the year is divisible by 100 then it's only a leap year if the year is also divisible by 400. So, the year 2000 was a leap year but the year 1900 wasn't."

"Is this getting us anywhere?" asked John.

"I think so," David continued. "Every month contains the dates 1 through 28, so the odds of any of these dates being the date are 12 in 365, or 0.03287-ish, according to my calculator. Or, to put it another way, about 33 in a thousand. For 29 the odds are 11 in 365, because February has 28 days, so the odds for 29 are 0.0301, or 30 in a thousand."

"So, the answer's 29?" asked Sharon, "aren't the odds the same for 30?"

"They are," replied David, "unless we factor in leap years. If I ignore the century rule, which is insignificant anyway, I need to do the odds over four years, not one. Three times 365 plus 366 is 1,461. Over four years there will be forty-five 29s and forty-four 30s. The odds for 29 are therefore 0.0308, or 31 in a thousand. The odds for 30 are 0.0301, or 30 in a thousand. I think that the answer's 30."

"Just to be pedantic, what are the odds for 31?" asked John.

"There are only eight months with 31 days so that's thirty-two in four years, which is 0.0219, or 22 in a thousand. It must be 30, sir," David responded.

"OK. So, we have ten days to get ready for the next murder. It looks pretty damn certain that the MO will be the same, but there are too many potential locations that have water to make this useful. I think we need to focus on the latest victim. What can we dig up on him? If we're lucky, maybe this wasn't just a random killing."

Investigations into Robert Jones had found nothing of interest. He was retired and lived alone. He worked as a line manager at the Birdseye factory in Ladysmith Road until it closed in 2005, which is when he retired. He had previously had several jobs, including a stint in the army in the 1970s. They had not recovered his mobile phone and his landline history had few calls, all of which were innocuous. It was looking like he was a random victim after all.

It was now 30th August. John was waiting for the inevitable phone call. It didn't happen. He arrived at the incident room at 8 am on 31st August.

"Good morning."

"Good morning, sir"

"Where's Sharon?"

"She was called away a few minutes ago. Another body has just been found."

Sharon returned to the room. "A body was found by a dog walker in the lake at Cleethorpes Country Park at around 7:15 this morning. The area's been cordoned off and SOCO are on their way. It looks like the body has been in the water all night."

Just then John's phone pinged. "Right on cue," he said. He opened the text and read it out loud.

"Use the clues you already have. Try to think like the FBI. On the 10th anniversary of the fire, the consequences will be dire."

"He thinks he's a bloody poet this time," said Paul.

"I think I know who it is, sir," said Sharon. "It's the guy who used to write those ridiculously impossible clues for that Dusty Bin program. You know, sir. 3-2-1."

"Ok. Let's calm down. We managed to decipher the previous clues, let's figure out what this clue means," said John. "Let's recap the previous ones."

"'The first murder was as easy as pie but had no point' led us to 3."

"'The second murder will be perfect' led us to 6."

"'The third murder will almost be worth its weight in gold' led us to 19."

"'The odds on the fourth murder are thirty in a thousand' led us to 30."

"So, we have 3-6-19-30. How does that help?"

"Maybe it's a combination for something?" suggested Julie.

"I think it's a date," said David. "3rd June 1930."

"That's a hell of a long time ago. Before any of the victims were born, even," said Sharon.

"It does look like a date though. I'd never thought of this before. Did anything of note happen on 3rd June 1930?" asked John.

After a considerable period of searching for that specific date, they had to confess it had led nowhere.

Then Paul spoke. "Maybe it's 6th March 1930? He said to think like the FBI. In The States they reverse the month and day, so 3-6-1930 is 6th March 1930. Can we check that date?"

David quickly Googled 'what happened on 6th March 1930'. He found that the first result returned was curious. He read it out loud.

"Packaged frozen food was sold in supermarkets for the first time, with an introduction of Birdseye products in 18 stores in Springfield, Massachusetts, United States."

"Wasn't Robert Jones a manager at the Birdseye Factory on Ladysmith Road?" he continued.

"Yes, he was," John replied. "Let's assume that this is the connection with the previous clues. What can we construe from 'On the 10th anniversary of the fire, the consequences will be dire'? What happened 10 years ago that fits in with the Birdseye clue?"

"The fire," said Sharon.

"What fire?" asked John.

"There was an arson attack on the Birdseye Factory sometime after it had been closed. David, can you check the date?"

It took David a couple of minutes before he replied. "The arson attack took place on 12th September 2007. The factory was destroyed. A couple of lads were arrested for arson but no charges were ever brought against them or anyone else."

"It fits," John said. "The 10th anniversary of the fire is in 12 days. Has he told us the date and maybe the location this time?"

"The factory isn't there anymore. Maybe we're off on a wild goose chase?" said Sharon.

"What did they replace the factory with?" asked John.

"Houses," Sharon replied. "I have a friend who lives in one of them". "I still reckon it's the Dusty Bin bloke," she muttered under her breath.

"OK. Let's recap," John said. "The texts lead us to a date – 6th March 1930. The only thing of merit we can find that happened on that date is that Birdseye first sold frozen food. The one victim we can identify used to work for Birdseye, in the factory on Ladysmith Road. The said factory burned down on 12th September 2007. The 10th anniversary of this happens in less than two weeks, which fits the final text. What do we think?"

"Why is he telling us? What does he gain by giving us clues?" asked Paul.

"The first clues were too vague to action," suggested David. "He told us the date, in a roundabout way, but there was no way we could have used this to stop the murders. I think he was just giving us the date to use for the final clue. It's this final clue that's the important one. He's not only given us a date but also possibly a location. Where the old Birdseye factory stood. I think he always wanted to be caught, but not until after he'd committed the murders."

"OK. This is what I want us to do," said John.

"Sharon, let's see what SOCO come up with from the latest crime scene. My guess is nothing, but you never know. We also need the results of the post-mortem when they are available, but I think we all know what the cause of death will be."

"Paul, let's assume that the killer is going to try and do something on 12th September at the location of the old Birdseye factory. We need to have observers in place as soon as we can. It could be that the killer will scout out the area before the 12th. We need to be ready to pick him up on or before the 12th so let's make sure we have officers on hand, including an ARV. We need to keep marked vehicles and uniformed officers away from the area in case they spook him."

"David, I want you to repeat the analysis of the texts to make sure our thinking is watertight. Have we missed something? Have we misinterpreted something?"

"And everyone, we need to continue to try and identify the victims. Now we have the Birdseye angle is there any way we can connect the unknown victims with Birdseye or the old factory?"

It was 12th September 2017. The 10th anniversary of the Birdseye factory fire. Unmarked police cars were dotted around the Ladysmith Road area where the factory used to be. It was now a waiting game. At 6:30 pm someone tapped the window of one of the unmarked cars. The policeman wound down the window.

"What do you want?" asked the policeman.

"I think it's more a question of what you want," the man replied. "I suspect that you are waiting for me to make an appearance."

"Why's that?" the policeman replied. He wasn't sure whether this was just some guy trying it on with the police.

"Because of the texts," came the reply.

The policeman exited the car and cuffed the man. He then read him his rights and placed him in the back of the car. The driver radioed in. "I think we've got him. We're bringing him into the station now."

The man was checked in by the desk sergeant before being escorted to an interview room. He was known to the police and had a criminal record for minor offences. His name was Tommy Flynn.

A duty solicitor was called in to accompany Tommy during his interview. It was 8 pm by the time that Sharon and Paul entered the interview room. The interview was being recorded on audio and video.

Sharon and Paul introduced themselves as the investigative officers on the murder cases and told Tommy that they were going to ask him some questions. At that point, Tommy spoke.

"Where's the lead investigator? John I think he's called."

"He's not here," Sharon replied, "Paul and I are assigned to this case and will conduct the interview."

It was true that John was not at the police station. Attempts to contact him on his mobile had been unsuccessful. A marked car had been sent to his address to pick him up but he wasn't there.

"Are you Sharon?"

"Yes."

"I have a message for you. Have you checked your mail?"

"What?"

"Have you checked your mail?" Tommy repeated.

Sharon quickly checked her email inbox and spam folder but found nothing of interest. "There's nothing there."

"Check the post, not your emails," Tommy responded.

Sharon left the room and checked for any post addressed to her. There was nothing. She then went to the front desk and spoke to the officer on duty. A large envelope had been delivered by courier addressed to her just after 8 pm that evening. On the back of the envelope was typed "open in front of witnesses." She took the envelope and returned to the interview room.

"Good, you found it," Tommy said, "I'm told to tell you that you should open it now."

Sharon opened the envelope. It contained six sheets of A4 paper. She quickly scanned the content. The first page was a cover letter of some sort, the remaining five pages seemed to be dossiers on five different men including an old photo of each. They were all wearing military uniforms."

"I'm told you should read the letter out loud for the benefit of the cameras," Tommy said.

Sharon started to read.

"Enclosed with this letter are dossiers on five men. You should recognise the first four men as the victims of the four murders you are investigating. The fifth man should also be familiar to you. You will see from the dossiers that each man is guilty of committing a war crime. It has taken a long time to track them all down but they have now paid for their crimes. Justice has been served."

"The man sitting in front of you is not the murderer. He is following my instructions. I have paid him for his services. He has never met me and will not be able to lead you to me."

The letter was unsigned.

Sharon and Paul stared at each other for a moment before examining the five dossiers. Although the photographs were old it was possible to identify that they were the four victims. But who was the fifth man?

"It's John!" shouted Paul, "he's killed John. That's why we can't find him!"

Paul left the room in a hurry. He needed to start the search for John. Sharon stayed with Tommy and was about to ask a question when her phone pinged. She had received a text. She read it.

"Go to where the tallest landmark used to be. Where, unlike your boss, things used to be whiter than white. You'll find the fifth murder victim there."

She left the room, caught up with Paul, and showed him the text.

"He must mean The Dock Tower. That's easily the tallest landmark around here," Paul said.

"No," said Sharon. "He said it used to be the tallest landmark. I think I know where he means. We need to go to the site of the old British Titan factory on the Humber Bank. The chimney there was taller than The Dock Tower. They demolished it a couple of years ago. Let's go."

Sharon spoke with David and asked him to stay with Tommy. She then set off with Paul.

Several police cars converged onto the old British Titan site and after a 20-minute search John's body was found. The MO was the same as the others, a puncture wound at the base of the skull. SOCO and the forensic pathologist were called in.

About two miles along the coast on the Humber Bank wall, a man observed the police presence. He broke a mobile phone by stamping on it and threw the remains of the phone over the wall into the sea. He then walked to his car, a silver BMW 5 series, got into the driver's seat, and drove away. His job was done.

About an hour later Sharon and Paul returned to the police station. They headed to the interview room where they relieved David.

Tommy was interviewed three times over the following 24-hour period, but his story stacked up. He was with Sharon when she received the final text, ruling him out as the texter. More significantly, it was confirmed that he was being held in custody in Hull for assault when one of the victims was murdered. The assault charge had later been dropped.

Tommy was able to show the texts he had received from the killer. These confirmed the instructions he had been given, including where to find £500 in cash. The cash had been confiscated when he was checked into custody. There was no forensic evidence on the notes to identify the killer. The notes had been in circulation for some time and could not be traced.

It appeared that Tommy was just someone that the killer had paid to distract the police. Tommy hadn't committed a crime and there was nothing to charge him with. At 7 pm on 13th September, just before the 24-hour deadline for charging or release was reached, Tommy was released from custody.

Tommy walked from the police station to the Tesco car park half a mile down the road. He got into the front passenger seat of a silver BMW 5 series that was parked there. He looked at the driver and spoke.

"Where are we going now?"

"Do you like Scotland? We have a job in Edinburgh," the driver replied, smiling.

"I like whisky," Tommy replied. "By the way, I really liked those riddles you sent when you realised that John was the investigating officer. Maybe we could do something like that the next time?"

"We'll see," the driver replied. "We were just lucky that John was assigned the case. That made things fun."

"Yes. Serendipity," replied Tommy.

The driver started the car and headed off towards the A180 out of Grimsby. It was going to be a long drive north.

1994 - FA Cup Final. Chelsea were defeated 4-0 by Manchester United.

Come and Meet Some of My Neighbours

Graham Albeck (Papa G)

At number 20 lives my sister Sue,
Who used to feed the Lions at the zoo.

Next door to her lives young Pippa,
For three nights a week she works as a stripper.

Her sister, by the name of Suzie,
Goes out some nights dressed like a floozy!

At number 9 is a widow called Lorna,
Who waits for the Postman at the street corner.

At number 10 live Dave and Carol,
Who make home brew cider in a barrel.

At number 4 lives busty Linda,
Without any curtains at her bedroom window!

A new couple's just moved in at number 30,
Where the front garden looks very dirty.

At number 15 lives Mr. Kelly,
Spends every night watching telly.

I'd like to try and have a date,
With Christine who lives at number 8.

In the corner shop works Indian Pasha,
Cor, now she's what you call a real smasher!

Her next to me, I'll call her Ann,
Keeps her house all spick and span.

The spinster at number 7, her name is Bobbie,
Knits baby clothes for a hobby.

I once had a neighbour by the name of Daisy,
Who played loud music that drove me crazy.

Number 12's now empty cos there lived Lottie,
Whose gone and moved to Lanzarote.

Afterword

Jackie Collins
(Current Grimsby Writers' Leader)

Firstly, thank you for buying *30 years of Grimsby Writers*.

We asked our longest-serving member and our newest member to create the Prologue to this book, by expressing their thoughts and feelings on Grimsby Writers.

I would describe the group as like-minded people who enjoy writing and sharing their work. We have members who have degrees in creative writing and members who have not written since school days. We are all on our own writing journey. Some are out for a fun trip on the steam train and some are on the arduous road trip to publication. We are all at different stops (stages) on our journey (in our development). In this book, each of us presents to you the best we can from the stop we are at.

Get a cuppa, or something stronger if you prefer. Sit comfortably in your favourite reading chair and journey with us through the stories in this book. We hope you enjoy them.

To anyone who has an itch to write, come along and meet us. Your first workshop is free. Or ring/email for a chat about your writing.

Meet at

Scartho Community Hub

St Giles Avenue
Scartho
Grimsby
DN33 2HB
Every Other Monday (Check dates)
2-4pm
For further information, contact Jackie Collins on: -
07981685147
jacqueline.collins@ntlworld.com

We would like to thank:

Simon J. Wood, a member of Grimsby Writers, for kindly formatting and publishing *30 Years of Grimsby Writers*. Simon J. Wood (website: tocutashortstoryshort.com) co-leads St James Writers with Sharon Taylor. They meet weekly on Wednesday evenings at the St James Hotel, Grimsby, from 7 to 9 p.m. www.facebook.com/groups/1598720047373833/

For the cover art, Magda Ehlers on Pexels.com

Lincolnshire's published authors, always so generous with their knowledge, time and talent to help us improve our writing.

All who contributed to *30 years of Grimsby Writers*.

Printed in Dunstable, United Kingdom

68396181R00068